SHOWDOWN IN GUN TOWN

Center Point
Large Print

Also by Lauran Paine and available from
Center Point Large Print:

Reckoning at Lansing's Ferry
Winter Moon
The Texan Rides Alone
Terror in Gunsight
The Story of Buckhorn
Absaroka Valley
Cheyenne Pass
Deadwood Ambush

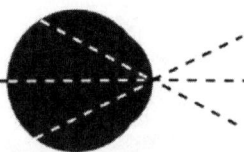

SHOWDOWN IN GUN TOWN

A CIRCLE V WESTERN

Lauran Paine

CENTER POINT LARGE PRINT
THORNDIKE, MAINE

This Circle Ⓥ Western is published by
Center Point Large Print in the year 2020 in
co-operation with Golden West Literary Agency.

Copyright © 2020 by Lauran Paine, Jr.

First Edition
December 2020

Printed in the United States of America
on permanent paper.
Set in 16-point Times New Roman type.

ISBN: 978-1-64358-745-5

The Library of Congress has cataloged this record
under Library of Congress Control Number: 2020943869

SHOWDOWN IN GUN TOWN

CHAPTER ONE

There are hundreds of ways for a man to ride into trouble. Ordinarily though, the man himself has something to do about it in each case, but not always; not when he came winding down out of the Saginaw Mountains as Walt Hodge did on that blistering summer day, slouching along toward the town of Sunflower, northernmost village of Huachuca County, Arizona, with nothing further from his thoughts than trouble.

Walt was thinking of a bait of grain for his horse at the Sunflower livery barn and a tall glass of cool beer for himself at some village saloon. He had never before seen Sunflower, Arizona Territory, in his life. Pacing southward away from those stiff-standing mountains, out across a long level stretch of cowed and heat-punished countryside, he peered from beneath a hat brim tugged low and saw nothing at all to be troubled about.

Sunflower was in the middle of a great, mountain girted plain. Almost any other time of year it would have looked inviting, even pretty, because, although it was clearly a cow town, it nevertheless had been squatting out there in Sunflower Valley for a long time. It had shade trees along its main roadway, and it had cool shadows somewhere roundabout nearly any time of day. It was a pleasant seeming, comfortable, and inviting town, which is all Walt Hodge thought of it as he scuffed through Main Street's ankle-deep tawny dust, turned in at the livery barn, and stepped down to toss his reins to an idling hostler.

"Grain him," he said, flipping over a cartwheel silver dollar. "Put him in a cool box stall and give him all the hay and water he wants."

Slowly he walked out into the weighted heat, looked left, looked right, picked out the Dallas House Saloon and went across to it. Nearly opposite the Dallas House, next to the Sunflower Savings Bank, was another saloon. This one's bold black overhead letters proclaimed it as **THE CAPITAL VARIETY HOUSE**. There were other saloons the length of Main Street as well as innumerable business establishments of other kinds, including a bake shop, a large general store, a gunsmith's shop, a saddle shop, and two land offices. They lined Main Street facing one another east and west, but from the listlessness of the town as Walt hiked on across to the Dallas House, it didn't appear that much business was being transacted in any of them.

Inside the Dallas House though, there were quite a number of men. It was not a noisy crowd. Men mopped off sweat at card tables, over at the bar, and along the front wall where they simply sat nursing a glass of beer in exchange for the privilege of sitting somewhere, anywhere, that outside hurting heat would not find them. At least that's how it seemed to Walt Hodge.

Even the bartender, a raw-boned, pale-eyed, and fiercely mustachioed individual, seemed wilted. His shirt front was soggy, his cheeks were red, and his non-committal gaze was milky with dispassionate disinterest in this solidly put together stranger who bellied up and said: "One cold beer, if you've got it."

With no conversation and a minimum of effort the barman drew Walt's drink, pushed it at him, and leaned upon his bar top sucking his teeth, staring steadily and sightlessly out into the dancing roadway.

"Hot," said Walt, sipping. "I just came down over those northward hills and it's thirty degrees hotter here than up there."

The barman's eyes grated in their sockets as they swung to consider Walt. They seemed to become mildly interested.

"Been like this for near thirty days now," the barman said. "All it'd take to send this whole blessed country up in smoke would be one dropped cigarette . . . one spark off a spur rowel." The barman reached for Walt's emptied glass.

Walt said: "No more. One's enough for now." He half turned, ran an indifferent glance over the room where all those listless riders and merchants sat, turned back, and studied the barman.

"Makes for short feed and dry water holes," he said.

"Yeah. It also makes for short tempers, stranger. You can almost feel it in the air. Sort of like electricity."

Walt left the Dallas House to amble over toward the Sunflower Hotel. There were a number of things a man fresh off the trail wanted when he hit town: cool beer and a bed up off the ground were usually the first two, and usually in that order.

He got a room, went up to it, and cleaned up after removing his shirt. He scrubbed himself, put the shirt back on, and returned to the shimmering roadway to stroll along in the shade of the overhang to study Sunflower. He wound up on the same side of the road as the livery barn, checked in there to see how his horse was faring, then passed along to the Capital Variety House, which was several doors south of the barn and nearly opposite from the Dallas House, being several buildings southward. Here he went in, noticed the same listlessness among the saloon's idling patrons, and headed over to the bar.

A thick-set man over by the saloon's roadside front window turned and watched as Walt halted, nodded at the barman, and said: "Cold beer."

Then the thick-set man came completely around, his gaze even and steady.

"He don't want no beer in here," that man said quietly, his words carrying easily to every man in that sweaty room.

Walt turned, measured the thick-set man, read the leashed violence in that rough, bronzed face, and seemed both puzzled and careful. He sensed rather than saw all the other masculine faces in the room turning to look him up and down. He was reasonably certain he'd never before seen that thick-set man; he knew for a fact this man was no particular enemy of his for two reasons. One, that tough face was totally unfamiliar. Two, Walt Hodge was new in Arizona. He was a Nevadan, in fact, who had trailed a band of eighty horses to Whipple Barracks for the Army. It had been his intention to loaf a little then head back to Nevada. He had a little money in the belt under his shirt and was therefore in no hurry to brave the fierce summer's scorch just yet.

After considering that thick-set man for a while, he said: "Mister, I think you made a mistake. I never saw you before in my life."

Behind Walt the bartender called over to the thick-set man: "Who is he, George?"

"One of *them*," George shot back, holding Walt's full attention with his malevolent stare. "I seen him come out of the Dallas House a while back."

Walt saw the others in that room turn carefully attentive. One of those heretofore quiet men, a solidly muscular bitter-lipped man in his mid-thirties with a dusty Stetson on the back of his head and an ivory-butted six-gun lashed to his right leg, strolled forward for a closer look at Walt.

He said: "You aren't very smart, cowboy, walkin' in here figurin' we wouldn't know."

"Know what?" asked Walt, coming fully around, setting his back squarely to the bar, facing this bitter-lipped man and all the others.

"Maybe he doesn't know," said a lanky, slow-moving range man as he pushed up from one of the card tables. "Where you from, mister?"

"He knows," said George from back by his window. "He was in the Dallas House long enough. They put him up to this, Charley, sure as I'm a foot high."

The lanky, slow-moving man called Charley shrugged as though unconvinced. He walked over to halt beside the bitter-lipped man and put a mildly suspicious, interested gaze upon Walt.

"I asked where you were from?" Charley said again.

Walt switched his attention from the muscular man to Charley. "Not," he said evenly, "that it's any of your damned business, Charley, but I just rode down from Whipple Barracks."

The bitter-lipped man said softly: "Yeah? And

what were you doin' up there? Bet you were tryin' to get the Army to come to Sunflower Valley and save old Bricker's hide."

Walt saw the disbelief in that man's gaze before he even answered, so he said nothing for a while. The more these men talked though, the less sense anything they said seemed to make, but right now Walt wasn't concerned with whatever was troubling them; he was concerned only with the clear fact that a fight was imminent here in this strange saloon, this strange town, and with these strange men.

"Well," said the bitter-lipped man, his face turning bleak even as his voice went softly flat and menacing. "What do they want from us . . . trouble? Or did they just figure because they hired a new man they could send him over here to spy and listen, and we wouldn't catch on?"

"Mister," said Walt quietly, "I got no idea what you boys are talking about. I just hit this town. I delivered a herd of horses to Whipple Barracks from Nevada. If you got a fight going hereabouts, I'm not in it at all."

The lanky, slow-moving one cocked his head a little and spoke to the bitter-lipped man without taking his eyes off Walt. "It could be like he says, Mike. Don't seem reasonable he'd walk in here free as you please, if he knew we were waitin' in here."

"Like hell," growled the man called Mike. "It's

too much of a coincidence. They want to know if we're all over here, Charley. They want to know if we're goin' to do anything when Bricker rides in."

The other men in that room began to crowd up behind Mike, growling agreement with this. From back by the window where he'd evidently been keeping a vigil, that thick-set one named George, spoke out.

"Forget him. It's too late for him to carry back any information anyway." Stiffly, George was standing over there with his back to the room and his bronzed, square-jawed face looking toward the roadway. "Bricker's coming now. Coming from the north with two of his hands ridin' with him."

Two of the range men toward the back of the room swung about and hiked over to join George at the window, but Charley and Mike and one other man still had Walt boxed in. They'd heard, he knew, and were pushing toward some swift decision about him before turning their backs. He thought he saw the growing look of violence in Mike's bitter-lipped face. This would be the man who acted, among them all, this Mike. Walt shifted his stance the slightest bit.

"Easy," he told Mike. "What I told you is the truth."

From out in the dancing roadway three horsemen approached, their rhythmic clop, clop,

clop the only sound until someone over in the direction of the Dallas House let off a derisive, hooting call. That cry seemed to trigger Mike. His right hand blurred hipward.

Walt Hodge's right arm was still back upon the bar top. He had no time to draw; his right fist though came forward straight as an arrow with his twisting full weight behind it. Mike's gun was half clear of leather when that sledging blow struck. Mike's arms flew out, his eyes rolled up aimlessly, and he dropped to all fours and hung there with his body sagging.

Walt rushed the slowly moving Charley, knocked him off balance, drew his gun, and backed off as the others came around looking dumbfounded. Off to one side the barman had both hands below his high counter.

"Don't try it!" Walt called to him. "You bring up a shotgun from back there and I'll start culling your customers out."

Lanky, slow-moving Charley had regained his balance. "Never mind," he said to the barman. "You can't buck this set-up. Put your hands in plain sight . . . empty."

The barman obeyed, and Charley, cocking his head over to one side in what appeared to be a characteristic of his, said tartly: "All right, mister, you've got the drop. But if you figure to march us out where Bricker can open up on us, you're out of luck."

15

The man called Mike groaned, shook his head back and forth, and clawed at the bar as he got back upright. Walt took one more rearward step in order to include Mike in his vision.

"Toss away your gun," he ordered Charley, which Charley did.

"Fine," Walt commented. "Now, go among your friends and disarm them too."

Charley didn't move. "Then what?" he asked.

"Then I'm getting the hell out of here," answered Walt. "Get on with it, Charley."

CHAPTER TWO

Charley obeyed. Of all the men in the saloon he seemed to be the only one who put any faith in Hodge's words. When he flung down the last gun, he straightened around and waited. When Walt didn't at once move, Charley jerked a thumb toward a closed door at the back of the room.

"That leads out into the alley," he said.

Walt edged along to that door, opened it, shot a fast glance rearward, eased down the hammer of his gun, and said: "Charley, I don't know what this is all about, but your friends here jump to conclusions too fast." He backed out of the saloon, slammed the door, and spun away toward a second door which led out into the alleyway. There, Walt ran swiftly along to the livery barn's rear entrance and jumped inside.

Beyond, out in the bitter sunlight, the town was as still as death. Up near the barn's front opening a man was standing just far enough back not to be seen and yet close enough so that he could see out.

Walt came up through the muffling run-way dust behind this man and said: "Get my horse."

That hostler gave a gasp and a little jump, landing down again half turned toward Walt. He was white to the eyes. He swallowed

17

several times before color returned, then he said peevishly: "Damn it all, mister, you shouldn't ought to sneak up on folks like that."

The liveryman was starting away, looking worried and irritable when Walt halted him.

"Who's Bricker?" he demanded.

Instead of answering, the hostler raised an arm pointing over toward the Dallas House. "Just went inside over there," he muttered.

"I know that much!" Walt exclaimed. "What's going on around here?"

The hostler lowered his arm, stared a moment at Walt, then, with a dolorous wag of his shaggy head, said: "Trouble, mister. Bad trouble."

That's all he would say. He continued on down through the aromatic barn for Walt's horse. While he was gone, Walt went up where the hostler had been standing and looked over at the Dallas House. There was no sound coming over those bat-wing doors. No men were visible over there, either, but at the hitch rack out front stood no less than seven saddle horses. It was a normal enough scene. *Too normal,* he thought, and stepped back as the liveryman brought up his animal, saddled, bridled, and ready to go.

"If I was you," mumbled the hostler, "I'd head out through the back alleyway. Hell could bust loose here any second, mister. A fellow ridin' out into that roadway might stop the first slug."

Walt had already made up his mind about the

route he'd take out of Sunflower so he stepped up over leather, turned his animal, and rode on down through the barn and out into the punishing blast of the sun beyond. There, he reined northward because it was the only direction he was familiar with, and passed along out of Sunflower.

He felt resentful more than angry as he went back along his earlier route toward those shimmering foothills. He'd gotten his drink of cool beer and he'd come within an ace of sleeping up off the ground too, but that was all he'd accomplished back at Sunflower except to walk with both eyes wide open into the middle of someone's feud.

Once, he halted a mile out and listened, but no gunshots, no loud noise of any kind came up from the town out to him, so he resumed his onward way.

"To hell with that place," he growled at his horse. "If this is any sample of what Arizona's like, the folks who live here can have my share."

Near the first thrust of mountains he angled along westerly toward an inviting fringe of red-barked pines.

He crossed a gravel ford where once water had leached color from the rocks leaving them bone-gray, followed up this withered waterway into the trees, and there unexpectedly came upon a little spring. Here, with trampled soggy ground all around where cattle, horses, and upland game had left their mark, he stopped dead still. This seemed an unlikely place to find water, here on the southward slope of the craggy old Saginaws, but no wanderer ever accepted good fortune more gratefully. He got down, let his horse drink, then waited a moment and tanked up too.

After all that had happened he stood in there hidden from sight gazing back down that sun-blasted land, turning the events and the words over and over in his mind. Whoever that bitter-lipped man named Mike had a grudge against—along with his running-mates Charley and thick-set George, and the others at the Variety House—was in real danger. Walt had lived with violence too long not to recognize its markings now, even in a strange place, when he saw them.

He tried to recall the men at the Dallas House. They hadn't seemed fired-up when he'd had his first drink there. And Bricker, whoever he was—Walt hadn't even seen him—must be, Walt now thought, a real ring-tailed roarer to get those other ones so keyed-up and triggered for battle just by riding into Sunflower.

He went over where resin-scented hot shade lay thick, tossed down his hat, and leaned upon a rough tree trunk. He hadn't even had time to get a meal in that lousy town down there. Not even a sack of tobacco, either, and he'd been out of smokes for three days now. None of these things, though, bothered him by itself. It was all of them combined, plus the hard looks and rough words that had been growled at him, that turned him belatedly grumpy as he stood in gloomy shade looking down his back trail.

He was so absorbed with his unpleasant thoughts that at first he was conscious of a fresh sound close by without really heeding it. Gradually then, he drew up off the old pine listening to the approach of a ridden horse, and because he'd already been through so much and was feeling irritable, he stepped around the pine tree moving onward toward that sound. If, for some reason, Mike or Charley or one of those others from the Variety House had somehow followed him, had somehow slipped around, and was now dropping in behind him, this time Walt was going to do the hard looking and rough talking.

Horse and rider came across a buck-run where fierce sunlight caught them, and passed over into the initial shade where that little spring was.

Walt saw the rider's upper body bend a little and straighten back again. It was a girl! He let her dismount over at the spring and half turn until she saw his indifferent horse standing a few feet off, saddled and drowsy, then he let her quick, wide glance whip over and halt fully upon him. She stood entirely still and unmoving; he had startled her, that much was obvious, but more

21

than that he caught a brief glimpse of something that seemed like shock, like sudden, explosive fear, in her liquid gaze. Then it was gone and she simply stood there staring over at him, looking as anyone might look who'd abruptly seen a stranger standing where no one would ordinarily be.

She wore a fawn-colored, split riding skirt and a blouse of a lighter shade. She had honey-colored hair caught up and held at the back of her head by a tiny red ribbon, and large smoky eyes that seemed to look through him in their wonderment and their searching.

"Hello," he said. "I thought you might be someone else."

"Hello," she said in a skeptical, careful tone, and lost enough of her initial surprise to study him and to consider his sun-darkened face carefully, his compact, powerful build that sloped from big shoulders down to a narrow waist, and afterward to loosen the reins at her horse's insistence so the animal could drink.

As she turned loose again, she said: "I didn't expect to find anyone here." She half turned to watch her horse suck up the cool spring water. "But I guess with water holes drying up like they are this summer, I should've known someone might be here."

"Yeah," he murmured, watching her profile, watching the lift and fall of her breathing. He came to a slow discovery—whoever she was, she was as lovely a girl as he'd ever seen.

"It's plenty hot all right," he went on. "And in more ways than one. Tell me, miss, do you live hereabouts?"

She looked up, swept her glance over him again, and motioned westward. "About two miles from here. I'm Leila Bricker. My father's Jim Bricker of the B-Back-to-Back outfit."

Walt stood a moment in speculative silence, before he said: "I see. I've heard that name before." He said this with just enough irony in his tone to catch her attention. He was about to say more when from behind him a man's quiet, menacing voice came out of the trees.

"Just stand easy, friend," said this unseen stranger. "Leila, toss away his gun."

The girl hesitated. She looked past Walt, then back again. She said: "I think he's all right, Carl. He was just as surprised to see me as we were to see him in here."

"Yeah? And why was he standin' back in there lookin' down toward town like he was waitin' for someone to ride along, maybe, so he could dry-gulch 'em? Naw, Leila, toss away his gun."

Walt waited, watching the lovely girl. His temper was rising. It showed on his face too, and she saw it when she started toward him. She paused as though to speak, but said nothing, reached down, lifted away Walt's gun, and

23

backed away as she tossed it down upon the pine needles.

The unseen man now strode forward, stepped around Walt, and grinned bleakly at him. This stranger was dark and wiry. He looked rough, capable, and willing.

He too saw Walt's anger and his grin broadened at sight of it.

"One of Mike Weedon's boys, aren't you?" he asked. "Waitin' for Jim to ride by on his way to town so's you could ambush him."

"Mister," said Walt in a very thin tone, "I don't have any idea just what the hell's going on in your lousy Sunflower Valley, but I'll tell you this much . . . I'm sure getting tired of people accusing me of things and acting like they wanted a shoot-out with me."

The dark man's grin faded out a little. He stared hard at Walt as though tempted to wonder about him, then he got that identical expression Walt had seen on Mike's face down in town—that look of disbelief even before he'd heard Walt's story.

"You're a liar," he said gently.

"Maybe he isn't," spoke up Leila Bricker. "Maybe he just happened . . ."

"If he's a stranger," interrupted the dark man, "how'd he know about this spring? Naw, he was waitin', Leila. He's one of Weedon's crowd sure as the devil."

"I'm part of no one's crowd," Walt insisted as his dander rose. "But if you think I'm waiting in here for Bricker to ride by on his way to town, you two are way off on your timing. Bricker's already *in* town. He rode in just as I rode out."

Leila flashed a worried look at the dark man.

He in turn stared hard from beneath lowered, frowning brows at Walt. "Another damned lie," he muttered.

Walt's gaze hardened against this man. "Put aside that gun, friend," he said, "and call me a liar. I don't know Jim Bricker from Adam's off ox, but those as do know him spoke his name just before I left Sunflower. He rode in with two other men. So, mister whoever-you-are, I'm no liar."

Leila said: "Carl, he might be telling the truth. If Dad didn't stay close to the foothills he could've gone directly on into town." She hesitated before continuing. "But if he hadn't seen Dad, how would he know he had two of the riders with him?"

"That's not what's stickin' in my craw right now," Carl grumbled. "What I'm wondering is, if he's such a stranger hereabouts as he pretends, how does he know who your pa is, Leila?"

"Damn it," snapped Walt. "I just told you. I *don't* know Bricker. Someone in Sunflower said his name just before I rode on out."

The dark man's furrowed forehead grew more

deeply seamed. Suspicion exuded from him in solid waves and yet he seemed a little doubtful now too.

From at his side Leila said to Walt: "Who are you? What were you doing in here by the spring?"

"My name's Walt Hodge. I just rode in here to get out of the sun. I didn't know there was a spring here until I saw it." Walt drew in a big breath. "This dog-goned country's sure full of nosy people," he growled. "Miss, I just delivered eighty head of horses to the Army over at Whipple Barracks. I'm from Nevada . . . never been in your Arizona Territory before . . . and right now I don't believe I ever want to be in it again."

"You tell that story too smooth," said Carl. "Mister, I don't believe you and I don't like you."

Walt squared fully around toward the wiry, dark man. "That makes us about even then," he said.

Carl stared a moment, then dropped his shoulders and started to turn away. Walt, switching his attention back to Leila, had his lips parted to speak and didn't see it coming.

Carl spun on the balls of his feet and flashed outward with a rock-hard fist. Walt took that entirely unexpected blow alongside the jaw and went down without a sound.

Carl put up a hand at Leila's quick, astonished protest, blew on his knuckles, and gazed dispassionately at the unconscious man lying there.

"He's one of Weedon's men, I'm plumb sure of that. I think he just learnt a lesson. When he comes around . . . if he's got a lick of sense . . . he'll light out of the country without even lookin' back. Come on, Leila. Let's get back to the ranch."

As Carl started away, he spied Walt's horse. He went over, pointed the animal westward, and gave it a sharp slap. Walt's horse jumped out with a startled snort and lit down running hard.

CHAPTER THREE

The sun had moved around and was entering that shady place by the spring with a reddening, afternoon glow to it. As the light spread across the ground, Walt came to, rolled over, put both hands palm down, and straightened his arms. His head roared for a moment, but no longer than that. He got up onto one knee, gingerly explored his aching jaw, wobbled it back and forth, and saw his gun lying ten feet away.

He got up, retrieved the weapon, leathered it, and crossed to the spring. There, lying belly-down, he pushed his entire head under water, held it there for a moment, then lifted it to let the water drip off. This cleared his awareness but the ache in his jaw remained. He got up, found his hat, and went to where his horse had been. It was no longer there.

Beyond this little fragrant spot the dazzling brightness was altering away from its previous lemon-yellow, bitter brightness. Walt walked as far as the last shaft of tree shade and halted to look out and around. His horse was nowhere in sight. He ran an exploratory hand under his shirt to assure himself that the money belt was still there. He hadn't been robbed and as recollection returned, he thought he wouldn't have been robbed anyway.

But he'd surely been slugged hard and set afoot. He remembered Carl's dark, sneering face and his wiry build. He also, with more vividness, recollected Leila Bricker. It was difficult for him to believe she'd been part of that last phase; she'd acted out the part of an astonished person perfectly, when she'd first come to the spring. He had to grudgingly admire her for that. But the other thing—that treacherous blow when Carl caught Walt off guard—he didn't want to believe she'd known that was going to happen too.

He went back, picked up the tracks of his horse, and started out. Regardless of how willing he'd been before to leave Arizona to the Arizonans, he couldn't go all the way back to Nevada on foot, so he left the trees, the spring, the resin fragrance, stepped out where the nearby mountainside was, and began tracking his animal.

All the rolled-up shimmering heat which bounced off the mountainside came down over him with an almost physical force. He hadn't progressed a half mile before he wished he could duck his head in that spring water again.

For a mile, one of the longest miles he'd ever walked in his lifetime, he was under the pitiless heat, then another of those little pine groves appeared, and he ducked into it. There was no spring here, but his horse had also loitered in this shade for a brief while before going on westerly again.

He sat down, shook off sweat, removed his hat so drying perspiration would cool his head, and manipulated his sore jaw again with one hand. It made him feel no better to acknowledge that Carl, for all his wiriness, had a punch as solid as the kick of a mule. For a little while he sat in this pleasant, drowsy place, then got up to pass on westward again on the tracks of his saddle animal. But movement southward caught his eye and turned him motionless for as long as it took to see the dust made by a hurrying party of riders a goodly distance off.

He waited in the pine grove, unwilling to be seen by any other inhabitants of this valley, and turned a little as those horsemen swept along north-westerly. There seemed to be five or six of them. Putting together the little gleaned facets he'd thus far picked up, he decided that would be Jim Bricker and the men from the Dallas House, out there, perhaps heading for Bricker's B-Back-to-Back Ranch.

If that was so, he mused, then obviously there'd been no shoot-out down in Sunflower after all. He shrugged. The way he felt at that moment he couldn't possibly have shed a tear if there'd been a genuine massacre down in Sunflower. He stepped back out into the sun smash and went trudging along again, following those same shod horse marks once more.

Without being aware that the sun was very near to being snuffed out in its westerly descent by the towering crags on his right, Walt suddenly no longer felt the direct burn of that savage sun when he was another half mile overland. What kept him from noticing was the sight, far ahead in the heat-hazed distance, of a rambling set of ranch buildings. He halted to study those hull-down low and squatty darkened shapes and conjectured on whether or not his saddle horse had made for them. As he started onward again, he thought dourly that the horse, no doubt catching the scent of other horses and water, had gone down there.

That was when he noticed the sun was suddenly no longer up there, but had dropped over a distant spire. The heat though did not readily diminish. In fact, for an hour afterward it seemed to steadily increase as though the earth and the mountains, every rock and every bush, was sighing and giving back all the piled up store of heat daylight had burdened it with.

Sweat ran under Walt's shirt; it trickled down into his eyes; it made him more than just irritable, it made him mad clear through. Someone, he promised himself, was going to pay dearly for setting him afoot. He'd already made up his mind who that *someone* was too.

• • •

It took a long time to get close to those buildings because, although they seemed close, the more he trudged toward them the more they retreated before his advance. It was turning shadowy out over the southward land and the towering Saginaws were hazed with purple before he halted for the last time. The buildings had stopped running from him. They loomed recognizably close even through evening's puddling gloom. It was the Bricker Ranch. He saw that deeply burned big B-Back-to-Back where a juniper tree stood beside the wagon ruts leading into the ranch yard.

He went only as far as that juniper, then sat down again. He felt dehydrated, furry-tongued, and mean. His jaw still ached, but not as much as it had before. His eyes grated in their sockets. He sat there studying the network of pole corrals, the two huge barns, and the other outbuildings—a bunkhouse, a shoeing shed, a saddle house, and set apart from these other structures, the main big ranch house, which had a shaded verandah all around it.

B-Back-to-Back looked prosperous. He tried to imagine why a man who possessed all this would indulge himself in a feud with other men. He gave up thinking about that when two riders loped in from the north. The reason he forgot was because he recognized that fawn-colored riding skirt, and also the wiry build of the second horseman. His lips drew out thinly, sardonically, at sight of those two.

He watched until they disappeared into one of the immense barns and a little later emerged on foot—Leila walking on toward the main house, the dark man called Carl ambling over to the bunkhouse.

Night fell swiftly. He rose up to draw back a deep breath of its wonderful coolness, listen briefly to the little normal sounds down there at B-Back-to-Back, and strike out through the thickening murk toward those barns and corrals. Somewhere down there, he was convinced, he'd find his horse. But he also had something else in mind. Still, he had to find the horse first. Aside from the money belt next to his hide, the saddlebags on that horse held everything in the world he owned.

He got into the yard without discovery, was almost across to the corrals when the supper triangle made its musical clangor. As men began drifting from the bunkhouse heading toward the cook shack, he slid out of sight behind a shed and remained there until he was certain no more men would be coming out into the yard.

Afterward, he got around one barn and down to the corrals. There, with much less searching than he'd considered possible, he came upon his saddled horse tied carelessly to a post. The animal turned, saw his shadowy figure emerge from the night, and softly nickered.

Now, he began considering that other notion in his mind. He took the horse to a trough, watered him, checked his rigging, found everything as he'd last seen it, and led the horse out and around the back to that distant juniper. There, after securing the beast, he returned once more to the ranch yard.

There was noise coming from the cook shack where men were noisily eating and talking. He was reminded of his own hunger while he maneuvered over next to the bunkhouse and blended into shadows there, by all those homely sounds, but hunger could wait. He'd been hungry before and he'd probably be hungry again, but right now he wanted something other than food, and yet, in its own way, also nourishing. He wanted to pay someone back for his aching jaw.

It was a long wait though.

Those B-Back-to-Back riders were in no hurry to depart from the cook shack. He could smell their tobacco smoke as he tried to make out the words of their rumbling conversation. He could not quite distinguish what was being said but the strength and vehemence of the voices told him nothing trivial was being discussed.

They began strolling out, finally. There were five of them. They crossed toward their bunkhouse leisurely, cigarette tips glowing and dying out as they advanced. He pressed in close where bunkhouse shadows were thickest, listening to booted feet strike harshly upon floorboards around front, and moved only when a door swung casually closed.

There was no moon. The stars cast only a very faint light. The corralled horses made little familiar sounds where they ate hay somewhere close by. Walt stepped to the very edge of the bunkhouse, tested the roundabout night, saw nothing to give alarm, pressed his shoulders flat, and sidled up to that closed door. Behind it, men's voices deeply rumbled. There seemed to be a card game in progress in the bunkhouse. He listened a moment, raised a hand, and braced himself with it.

"Hey, Carl!" he called out.

Inside, the voices winked out for a moment. Walt held his breath. They started up again. One man called for cards, another swore lazily at the cards he already had, and less than five feet from Walt's upraised hand the bunkhouse door swung open to spill orange lamplight out into the yard. A lean, wiry shape stepped forth.

Walt moved. He caught that peering wiry man by the shoulder, swung him violently around, and waited just the fraction of a second it took for Carl to recognize his assailant, then swung. He had his body twisted with that blow. Carl took it flush on the point of the chin. He was falling even before Walt let go and sprang away, back around the side of the bunkhouse.

He raced around the nearest barn and never once slackened speed as he made a big half circle around B-Back-to-Back's yard. Behind him, men's shouts and curses rose into the hushed night. When he dared, he halted to look back. They were standing over there with lamplight spilling over them looking from the sprawled, face-down figure of Carl, out into the quiet night, bewildered and anxious. The light abruptly went out. Walt saw no more, so he ran on to the juniper, got astride his mount, and loped off easterly, knowing those men could hear him now but also knowing he was beyond the range of a six-gun.

Once, a man's indignant shout rang down the night, but beyond that there was nothing.

He slowed a mile farther along, flexed his paining right hand, examined it closely, found no broken skin, and smiled. It was a pleasant kind of pain.

There had been green feed in tiny amounts back by that little hidden spring. So he made for that place again because his horse needed something to eat. It had been a long time since the animal had gorged at Sunflower's livery barn. In some ways it seemed that it had been years.

He eventually reined off into those familiar trees, off-saddled and hobbled his animal. As the horse hopped away to graze, Walt went to the spring and drank, bathed his face, and drank again. It was not so noticeably hot now, but the night was still a long way from being cool.

He wished for a smoke, for something to eat, and settled in the end for another long drink of spring water, and after that for a bath.

He lay back on soft pine needles feeling satisfied with himself. It gradually came to him, too, that by now it would be safe to slip back into Sunflower for something to eat. Before he got back down there it would be midnight; there would be an all-night café—there always was in a cow town—but more important, the men who had involved him inadvertently in their feud, would in all probability either be gone out of Sunflower and back to their ranches by now, or would be at one of the saloons. Either way, if he was careful, he could avoid them, but one thing he could not indefinitely avoid was the insistent growling in his stomach.

But he waited. The night was young, his horse hadn't grazed long, and he was in no big rush. He lay there gazing up through stiff-topped pines at the purple heavens, thinking of Leila Bricker. If ever another woman had so thoroughly and completely captured his attention before he could not now recall her.

Under less stringent circumstances, he told himself, he would want to know her. He plucked a pine needle, popped it between his teeth, and thought that even under these circumstances he wished he knew her. She had an aura that sang out to a man even from memory, a pulling power that drew a man's thoughts to her even though he had other things upon his mind, even though he had ample reason not to recall her kindly.

He pulled the pine needle from his mouth and tossed it before rising up and going over to begin rigging out his horse. But even as he did this, and afterward, even as he was riding down across the empty land again, he didn't think of Carl or Mike or Charley—he thought entirely about Leila Bricker.

Chapter Four

He was about a mile southward from the spring, bound for Sunflower and riding easy, when he caught the stealthy sound of riders. Instantly he was alert and interested. He stopped finally, far enough north from those horsemen to be unable to see them and too distant for them to see him. He considered their possible identity and purpose. They were riding northwest as though passing out from Sunflower. As though heading straight for B-Back-to-Back.

He knew it wouldn't be Bricker's men, because he'd left them at their ranch no more than an hour before. It did not seem likely they would be visitors. It was too late in the night for guests to call, and, besides that, there were no women along.

He thought it would be the Weedon bunch, and if this were so, then they were not paying Bricker any social call. He eased forward another hundred feet, harkening to the approach of those men. His horse pricked up its ears, also interested. Voices came desultorily, some sounding drowsy, some not, but all sounding resolute. He caught a little of what was being said. It confirmed what he suspected. That was Mike Weedon out there, leading his crew to B-Back-to-Back. They meant to force some issue Walt did not understand, but he understood what forcing this issue meant—an all-out attack upon B-Back-to-Back.

He heard someone say something tart about old Bricker and another man say something altogether different about Leila. That was when he decided to move. Those men out there owed him something too, the same as Bricker's man Carl had owed him something. He rode very carefully down-country as Weedon's bunch passed unsuspectingly ahead, and got in behind them. He would collect from this crew too.

Formless night was his valuable ally and the noise Weedon's men were making covered his cautious approach. The riders, six in number, were disorderly the way they poked along. They seemed in no hurry at all, which was understandable. The best time to strike an enemy was when he was the least suspicious, as when he was perhaps asleep in his blankets in the small hours of a moonless night.

But this very deliberation helped him. One of Weedon's men slouched along yawning from time to time. This one was a good twenty feet behind the others. Walt came even with this man with his head also dropped forward, with his hat brim hiding his features even though they were hidden by the night. He saw the cowboy swing a look over, then yawn prodigiously and look away again. The man didn't speak. They went along for perhaps a hundred and fifty feet like this before Walt's plodding animal inched over very close. Walt's stirrup struck the stirrup of the other man, bringing Weedon's rider to annoyed awareness.

He muttered—"Look where you're going, dammit"—and carelessly raised his head to shoot a look across. He had only one second to see that descending pistol barrel before it crunched down over his hat. He slumped forward.

Walt caught the man, steadied him for a little ways, until he disarmed him and flung away his weapons, then he halted the horse and rode on, leaving the man precariously balanced up there. The horse fidgeted. He didn't like those other animals walking off, but as the onward sounds and scents diminished he stood easy. Only when he dropped his head for a mouthful of graze did he upset that careful balance, dumping his unconscious rider.

Walt took this man's place at the tail end of Weedon's line slouching along, head hung, and all loose in the saddle. For nearly a half mile he made no move toward the next rider. When he did though, that second man turned, saw his horse hiking along with the reins loosely swinging, and growled at him.

"You better wake up, George. You go along like that and you'll be in old Bricker's yard before you know it."

Walt jerked his head as though suddenly wrenched out of sleep. He muttered at the man beside him, put up a hand, and covered his lower face in a simulated yawn. He had no hand upon the reins so his horse, responding to its rider's shifting weight, angled in closer to this second cowboy. This man, instead of growling when Walt's stirrup rubbed against his own stirrup, put out a hand and lightly jarred Walt with it.

"Wake up, George, you damned fool. We'll be up there in another half hour. Wake up and look alive." The cowboy chuckled. "I figured after this afternoon you'd be faunchin' at the bit for another crack at B-Back-to-Back." The chuckle died out. "One thing you got to hand that fellow . . . he had guts, bracin' the whole crew like he did and knockin' the tar out of Mike with one punch. You got to hand it to him. Charley told me he almost believed the fellow wasn't a Bricker man, until he got the drop on us and ran out. He also said Bricker's hirin' a better breed of gunslinger, or that one wouldn't have kept his word, he'd have marched the lot of us over to the Dallas House and made Bricker a present of the Weedon crowd unarmed." When he finished speaking, the cowboy wagged his head back and forth. "That'd been fatal, more'n likely, had he done that, George. You know? Hey, George, damn it . . . I'm talkin' to you. Wake up!"

Someone up ahead where the others were riding

twisted to say: "You know how to wake him up? Light a match and drop it in his boot."

At once several men chuckled.

The man beside Walt called back he just might do that. He turned and said: "You hear that, George?"

Walt nodded.

"Then, by golly, you'd better look alive."

There was no chance to catch this man off guard. He was not only wide awake, he was also talkative and constantly looking over. Walt dropped his right hand, palmed his six-gun, leaned from the saddle until his face was within inches of the cowboy's shoulder, pushed the gun barrel he held low into the man's ribs.

"Rein back, friend, and don't open your mouth," Walt whispered to the man.

The cowboy's astonishment was complete. His jaw fell, his eyes swung, and he instinctively reined back.

Walt straightened back in the saddle, waited a moment until the others were almost lost in the onward night, then said: "Loop your reins and turn your head to the right." When this order was obeyed Walt reached over, disarmed the cowboy, flung away his weapons, and brought his own gun barrel upward and downward in a short, chopping arc. The horseman gave a little sigh as he slid off his saddle as limp as a sack of grain.

Walt took the man's reins, stepped down, and

looped one of them around the cowboy's ankle. He wasn't being solicitous about leaving that cowboy afoot out there, he didn't want that horse to try and rejoin the others on ahead. Afterward he remounted and went along as before in the wake of Weedon's crew.

But now the opportunity of catching another rider lessened. They were no more than a mile from the Bricker Ranch.

A voice Walt recognized as belonging to Mike Weedon said: "Careful now, boys. I'm sure they won't be expectin' anything . . . but be right careful all the same."

At this admonition the loosely riding men closed up a little, turned silent and alert, and bunched up. One man looked back, made out Walt back there, and said softly: "Come on, you and George quit draggin'."

Walt, watching this rider from beneath his hat brim, saw the man's twisted form slightly stiffen, saw the cowboy's head lift a little.

"George . . . ?" the man called, his voice rising, breaking off. "Which one of you is that back there?" The cowboy's tone was turning faintly suspicious, slightly alarmed now. Others looked back.

"Someone strike a match," that onward rider said. "That doesn't look . . ."

"Hey, he's droppin' back!" another yelled.

Indeed, Walt was dropping back. He whirled

and hooked his horse and went racing northward. Over one shoulder he saw a match flare. Someone's voice was raised inquiringly behind that match for just a second before Weedon's corn-husk dry command rapped out.

"Kill that damned match, you fool!"

Walt stopped a long way out and listened. The voices were intermingled and bewildered sounding. One voice rose over the others; it belonged to the lanky, slow-moving man called Charley. Walt recognized it at once.

"Don't make sense," Charley was insisting. "If Bricker's out here, he wouldn't send in just one man." Charley paused, swore, then added: "I'll tell you who that was, confound it, that was the same fellow who got the drop on us at the saloon sure as hell."

"This proves he's a B-Back-to-Backer then," grumbled another rider. "What did he do with George and . . . ?"

"Shut up," snarled Mike Weedon's infuriated voice, breaking over all those other voices. "If it's just that one man . . . maybe this proves he isn't a Bricker rider. A couple of you go back, see if you can find George and Les. Sure as the devil he's been skulkin' along in our wake, tryin' to knock us off one at a time."

Walt heard two of the remaining men rein around and lope back the way the bunch of them had just come. He also heard Weedon say to the man called Charley: "I don't get this at all, Charley, damned if I do. He wouldn't be out here for B-Back-to-Back. Bricker wouldn't trust in just one man to get us, he'd fetch along his whole crew."

Charley did not reply.

Walt waited a moment longer before easing out westward, riding slowly and quietly. When he was well away from Weedon's bunch and approximately equal distance from the Bricker place, he drew his hand gun, tilted it skyward, and let off two quick shots.

The crashing explosions of those twin muzzle blasts alerted everyone within five miles that all was not well out in this gloomy night. Walt sat there calmly shucking spent casings and plugging in reloads confident he'd aroused everyone down at B-Back-to-Back. As he holstered his gun he lifted his rein hand, turned, and rode slowly on southward in the direction he'd been riding before any of this had come up.

After a while he caught the sound of other horsemen in the night. They were not riding fast but they were definitely riding away from the Bricker place. Walt smiled, figured the score evened, and paid no more attention to those bitter riders off in the east where Mike Weedon and his ham-strung crew were beating a retreat out of the upland country with their anger and their resentment. They knew as well as Walt knew, that somewhere behind all of them, Bricker and his armed men were scouting the countryside alert and suspicious about those two tell-tale gunshots.

Walt got within sight of the few, fitfully burning carriage lamps down by Sunflower before he halted to gauge the night again. He heard Weedon's crew preceding him into town and hung back until he was satisfied those tired and frustrated night riders had gone on. They wouldn't try another surprise this night. They would instead bed down with disgruntled bitterness.

He rode on into Sunflower an hour later using back alleys, left his animal in the dark behind a store, and walked on foot around to Main Street. The town was as silent and empty seeming as a graveyard. Up at the livery barn two lamps glowed. There was another light at the general store and still another one at a little all-night beanery wedged between two larger buildings. He made for that café, surveyed its worn old counter through a window before entering, saw only one customer in there—an elderly, grizzled person hunched around a cup of black coffee— and hiked on in.

The café man had a drooping Longhorn mustache, a respectable paunch, and dull-looking dark eyes. He studied Walt, nodded, mechanically

47

swiped at his counter where Walt eased down, and asked cautiously: "What'll it be, mister?"

"Steak and onions," answered Walt, "and a gallon of coffee."

The café man nodded and made a heavy, tired smile. "You must've been postponin' a few meals to be that hungry," he said as he turned and padded away.

The grizzled man farther along the counter turned, threw Walt a curious look, and upon his shirt front a deputy sheriff's badge caught lamplight and glinted.

"Come a long way?" the grizzled lawman asked, his tone professional sounding to match his interested stare.

"Far enough," Walt replied. "From over the Saginaws up at Whipple Barracks."

The lawman raised up to turn again and continue his assessment of Walt. He looked tired and pensive and somber, as though, if he'd ever known how to smile, he'd long since forgotten which muscles to use now. He was in his fifties, Walt thought, but powerfully built and seasoned. He would be a hard man when crossed even now, even in his sundown years.

"Was up that way myself," he said hollowly. "Just got back this evenin'. You wouldn't be the fellow who trailed a herd of Nevada horses down there, would you?"

"I would," answered Walt, and turned as the

café man ambled up with his coffee. "Eighty head. It was a tough drive at times."

"Reckon so," murmured the lawman. "I saw 'em. They were fine-lookin' horses."

Walt watched the fat man frying his steak in the kitchen. Until that rich fragrance filled the little café, he'd had no idea how completely hungry he'd been.

The deputy spoke again, catching Walt's attention anew. "Figurin' to hire out down here, mister?"

"No sir," Walt said emphatically. "As soon as I've eaten I'm heading out of your territory."

"In the night, mister?"

Walt thought he detected suspicion. He smiled up at the lawman. "Cooler traveling in the night," he said, and looked away.

CHAPTER FIVE

He rode out of Sunflower with the night nearly spent, feeling drowsy but replete and satisfied. He still didn't know what the feud between Jim Bricker and Mike Weedon was about, but neither did he care.

He rolled a cigarette with his reins looped, with his horse slogging along toward the lifting pass through the Saginaws. After he lit it, he deeply inhaled, exhaled, then he yawned. That steak lay like lead behind his belt buckle but it was a good kind of heaviness.

The sky was purple except where those little moth holes up there let light shine downward through its all-covering depth. The air was balmy even though dawn wasn't far off. Walt on his horse passed quietly along toward that pass leading out of Sunflower Valley, and it seemed that from here on, the road back to Nevada held no surprises and no additional troubles.

He paused once, far out, looking westward and idly speculating about the Bricker place, about Carl and those rough-looking riders down there, but mostly he speculated about Leila.

This was his private little tribute to her, this brief halt in the middle of the night-shadowed plain before the Saginaws loomed up. He thought wistfully of her beauty, of her promise, then shook out his reins and went as far as the little spring where he'd first seen her and halted there to await full daylight before tackling the nearby mountains again.

He let his horse wander with only a loosened cincha and a bridle slung from the saddle horn. He didn't off-saddle because he knew, from the appearance of the eastward rims, dawn wasn't far off. He meant to continue onward as soon as it was light enough to do so. For that reason too he didn't bother hobbling the horse as he dropped down to lie back for this little time and reflect upon the events of this momentous day.

He was still lying like that three hours later when a shod horse's solid footing sprang him wide awake with a thundering heart. With the sun high over those eastward peaks, he did not recall falling asleep at all but obviously he had because it was now nearly nine o'clock according to the location of that dazzling sun.

He whipped upright and swung toward that horse sound, his right hand dropping instantly, all in one blurred movement, but he was not quick enough, as a quiet voice spoke from in among the stiff-limbed pines behind him.

"I hardly expected you to be here again."

He saw her sitting her horse, watching him, her gray eyes level and wondering, her face settled in a kind of wry expression.

"You're lucky Carl isn't riding with me today."

He eased off a little, some of the stiffness going out of him at the sight of her, but not all of it. He very slowly turned one way, then the other way, looking out and around.

She shook her head, and said: "I'm telling the truth. He isn't with me today. As a matter of fact, he's back at the ranch not doing very much. You see, someone slipped up last night, called him from the bunkhouse, and almost broke his jaw." She gazed steadily down. "That wouldn't have been you, by any chance?"

"It was me," he said roughly to her. "You're lucky you're a girl or you might've gotten one too. I don't look kindly on slugging a man when you've tricked him into being off guard, miss."

"I don't either. I didn't know he'd do that. But maybe it taught you never to be off guard. At least this way, you'll remember. You realize, of course, that had it been a bullet you wouldn't be able to, would you?"

He stumped over close to where she sat her horse studying him. "That other little ruckus last night," he said tartly, looking fully into her eyes. "You could thank me for that if you were of a mind to."

Her brows came slightly together in puzzlement. "You mean . . . that was you who fired those two warning shots?"

52

"Yes, ma'am. I also salted down a brace of Weedon's boys."

She shook her head at him, that gray gaze turning smoky, turning to the solid grayness of an oak fire under a wintry sky.

"But . . . but you're a Weedon man," she said.

"Miss Leila," he said irritably, "I'm no one's man. I thought I made that clear yesterday before your friend slugged me. I went down to your ranch and got my horse back. Then I paid off Carl for what he did. I was going to Sunflower to get something to eat when I ran across this Weedon bunch riding for your place, and cut in behind them, knocked a brace of them over the head, fired those shots to let you folks know something was wrong, then went to town, ate a big steak, and headed back up here on my way out of Arizona Territory. That's the whole blessed story."

"But why?" she asked, with a drag of uncertainty to her voice. "Why did you warn us? Why did you fight those Weedon men?"

He lifted his shoulders and let them fall. "I owed them that much . . . just like I owed Carl a cracked jaw. Now it's over as far as I'm concerned."

She looked at him, her perplexity diminishing, her troubled mind seeming finally to relax. "You were telling the truth then. You weren't one of Mike Weedon's riders," she murmured. "But who are you?"

"Walt Hodge. I was just loafing along when all this erupted right in my face." He stooped, plucked a grass blade, and put it between his lips.

Everything either of them had to say to the other had now been said, but he didn't want it to end, so he said: "Tell me something, Miss Leila . . . just what's this whole she-bang all about?"

"You mean between my father and the Weedon bunch?"

He nodded, watching sunlight touch her hair and explode into silent glory.

"Well, it's not easy to explain, but in just a few words it's over range rights. You see, during dry spells Weedon has been drifting his cattle north. My father never said very much about that, although this upland country is our range. That was until this summer when even our grass was running short. He asked Mike to keep his herd south of town. Mike refused and pushed more cattle up here than he's ever done before. So you see?"

"Like looking in a mirror," he murmured, then cast away the chewcd grass blade, and wagged his head back and forth. "It's always the same, isn't it . . . when grass gets short or water holes dry up? Men start their feuding."

She seemed to harden against this remark and had an instant retort. "My father is a fair man. As I told you, he hasn't said anything to Mike until this year. But now we need every blade of grass desperately for our own beef. If you're any kind of a cowman, you'll know how that is."

"Sure," he said in the same wry tone, and departed from that topic. "Tell me something else, Miss Leila. What did your father aim to do when he rode into Sunflower yesterday?"

"Weedon had sent word he dared him to have a showdown." Her smoky gaze turned steely. "My father rode in after having our men drift in ahead of him and wait at the Dallas House. Weedon is capable of treachery. He wanted to be prepared."

"And?"

"When he got there Weedon's bunch had been at their favorite hang-out . . . the Variety House . . . but something had happened. They'd left all in a bunch just before my father got our men together."

Walt nodded, remembering how uncertain, undecided those men at the Variety House saloon had become after he'd got the drop on them.

He said: "You know, it's kind of uncanny how everything I've done so far has kept your father and this Weedon character from locking horns."

He told her of his arrival in Sunflower, of his close call at the Variety House. He concluded with: "I had no idea what it was all about. Not even when you and Carl jumped me here at the spring yesterday. Until you just now told me I still didn't know. And yet every time I've moved, it has upset someone's timetable."

She made a little rueful smile at him. "My father would thank you, if he knew. He doesn't want a range war."

"How about Carl?" he asked, stroking his jaw before he added something to this. "A man who'd do what Carl did to make his point is pretty low in my book, Miss Leila."

"No. You don't know Carl. He's our range boss. He'd do anything at all to protect our rights. It's the Indian in him, I guess, but he can't see anything but B-Back-to-Back. That's how he is." She stopped speaking suddenly, bent forward, and looked steadily at him. "But even if you're right about his being treacherous, you're no better. When he came around this morning, he said he'd recognized you . . . that you'd given him no chance at all." She straightened back again, having made her point. "Does one wrong make another wrong right?"

He stood there looking up at her intent, indignant expression, very near to smiling at her. "I reckon not," he conceded. "You're right. Only I guess sometimes folks just don't remember. All they remember is how things *are,* not how they *should* be."

She saw the softening of his gaze. It brought a changing expression to her lips. They lost the hardness and the stubbornness. They stood there considering one another for a long interval of total silence. Her smoky gaze darkened upon him and glowed, her breathing quickened, and suddenly she was not someone defending friends; she was a woman, lovely and desirous of being noticed.

He hauled half around to look southward out over the shimmering valley floor. There was a feeling in him he'd never before experienced.

She spoke to him from behind, her voice soft and rich and compelling. It was a weapon and whether she knew it or not he listened to every lift and fall of it.

"Will you come back to the ranch with me and talk to my father?"

"He's got a full crew, Miss Leila," answered Walt without facing back around. "Besides, this Arizona country doesn't exactly agree with me."

"It doesn't agree with anyone when there's trouble. It warps people. I've noticed the change in our riders just within the last month, since this thing began."

"Yeah," he murmured, thinking back a moment to her hot expression as she'd defended the range boss, Carl. "It's workin' on you, too." He faced her. "No thanks, Leila. I've seen range wars. They ruin people. They even ruin whole areas of the country."

With bitterness she said: "So you'll ride on. That's easiest, isn't it? You don't have to prove anything by doing that."

"Prove what?"

"That you're a man. That men sometimes are bigger and stronger than guns. Well, ride on then, Mister Hodge. That way you'll never have to prove to yourself whether you're the man you'd like to believe you are, or not."

He lunged, caught her bridle as she started to swing around, brought the horse down to a standstill, and stood close at her side, looking up. They were not far apart now. He watched closely and saw something come up in her eyes and catch fire. It was like a magnet drawing him, like a glimpse of blue light shining out of a darkness to him. He reached up and pulled her from the saddle, released her, and stood there, now seeing astonishment replace that fire in her eyes.

"I don't have to prove anything to myself," he said. "I told you I'd seen range wars. What I didn't tell you was that I've been through them." He looked over her shoulder, then back again. "That's why I'm footloose, Leila . . . a range war orphaned me. So don't tell me what I've got to prove to myself or disprove."

Her voice came low and husky in the face of his agitation. "I'm sorry. I couldn't have known that. But I'm sorry all the same."

He saw the erratic pulse in her creamy throat, watched the moving, strange things mirrored in the depth of that winter-day gaze of hers, and he also saw her lips loosen toward him. She dropped her glance but at once brought it back up to him.

Something confused and confusing had suddenly come into this little secret place with them. She was young, he was young, and whatever this strange thing was which was there with them, was new to both of them.

"I guess . . . ," he muttered, and let it die, whatever it might have been. He put out both hands, let them fall upon her waist, and tipped her up toward him. She didn't fight, but when their lips met, hers were cold, unresponsive, unresisting but putty-like in their coolness.

He pushed her away and flamed red. There was a bitterness to his mouth like acid, and fire points glowed in his gaze at her.

"Yeah," he murmured in that dry, dry tone he sometimes used. "All right. I apologize."

His pride was hurt, she knew that much, but something else in him had turned iron-like too. She didn't know what that was or even why it was, she only knew that it was.

She also knew something else. She'd felt her own hungers rushing up at him during that kiss and had fought them with her Bricker will, which was strong. But now she didn't want it this way at all, so she fumbled for her second chance. She reached for him, touched his chest, lay both hands flat upon him, and stood upon her tiptoes seeking his mouth. She kissed him like that, very tenderly, the fullness of her mouth holding him still until she dropped back down.

Then she turned, went over to her horse, stepped up, and without another glance rode on out of the pines to the burning plain beyond. There, while he watched without moving, without even seeming to breathe, she loped away westward.

CHAPTER SIX

Sunflower lay cowed and lifeless under the midday smash of the sun when Walt rode down its main thoroughfare as far as the livery barn. He left his animal there under the hostler's surprised stare and went along to the local constable's office.

When he entered this little drab building with its lingering odors of man sweat, horse sweat, and stale tobacco, he caught the lifting glance of that same grizzled deputy sheriff he'd met the night before. This lawman kept watching Walt for a space of some seconds before he squared around in the chair at his desk and made a careless gesture toward a wall bench. He'd recovered from his surprise, which had never really showed upon his weathered, darkened face, and was now awaiting the explanation he thought might be coming.

"Damned country's hotter than the hinges of hell," said Walt, as an opener.

"Yup," muttered the deputy. "Near as hot as Nevada. I put in four years up in the Washoe country when I was a young buck durin' the Indian troubles."

Walt removed his hat, tossed it upon a table,

and ran bent fingers through his curly mane. "I didn't head out, after all," he said.

In the same laconic manner the older man said: "So I notice. Something worthwhile change your mind?"

Walt seemed to drift off in his thoughts for a moment. "Worthwhile enough," he ultimately murmured. "Tell me, Deputy, just who is Mike Weedon?"

The lawman's expression smoothed out. He'd had a hunch before and this question had more or less confirmed it. It did not at once occur to him his hunch might be as thoroughly wrong as it was.

"Mike's a cowman south of town. He runs a lot of cattle. I think I know what's on your mind. Heard about it when I got back home last night. Mike and Jim Bricker got a little argument goin' over range rights in the uplands country. You're figurin', since you heard about this thing, to go hire your gun to Mike."

The lawman stopped speaking. He and Walt gazed steadily at one another for a long time, then Walt gently smiled and gently shook his head.

"Deputy, if you'd sat up all night trying to figure a better wrong answer than that one, you couldn't have done it."

"I see. Then you want to hire out to Bricker."

"Wrong again. What I want is to stop a range war before it even starts."

"Yeah? Why? What's your interest? You left town last night ridin' north toward the Saginaws. Who'd you talk to after you left here?"

Walt's smile lingered, turned teasing. He stood up. "I'll leave that for you to fret about, Deputy. Right now it's not important. What I'd like to know is how we can stop this thing before it gets going."

"We?"

"It's the law's job to prevent fights as well as move in after they've taken place, isn't it?"

"Sure, but what makes you think I need any help with this one?"

Walt went as far as the door, leaned there in the opening, and related to the deputy sheriff everything that had happened to him since he'd ridden into Sunflower the day before. When he was finished, he watched that grizzled, older man rummage for his tobacco sack, drop his head, and go to work manufacturing a smoke.

As the lawman worked, his expression ran a gamut of changes. He was thinking, and he was thinking hard. Finally he tilted back, lifted his faded, yeasty eyes to Walt, and lit up, blew outward, and shoved up from his chair.

"You can't go talk to Mike," he finally said. "If you did all you've just told me, he'd try for your hide on sight. I'll go talk to him."

The deputy turned, threw a hard look over,

and said: "You don't want to tell me why you're buyin' in, do you?"

Walt shook his head.

"I thought not," growled the lawman. "Well, let me explain something to you. . . ." The older man removed his smoke and sighed, staring over at Walt for a few seconds before saying: "What'd you say your name was?"

"Walt Hodge."

"Mine's Fred Wheeler. Let me explain something to you, Walt. Mike Weedon's trouble four ways from the middle if he's crossed. He hires tough riders and he drives a hard bargain. I didn't know the thing had gotten this far along. Oh, I heard a little about it before I went north, but this . . . this issuin' ultimatums to meet him in town and settle a difference . . . I had no idea it'd gotten that far."

The deputy punched out his cigarette, dropped the thing into a spittoon, and went on.

"But my position is simply this. I'm constable of this town by common election. I'm also an appointed deputy sheriff of the country. That's so's if I got to ride beyond the town limits to make an arrest I have the authority. But just where I'd be if I jumped smack dab in between Weedon and Jim Bricker . . . I'm not sure. So, for now, I think the wise thing is to do nothing at all."

Walt stared, nonplussed. He'd sized up this

rough-seeming old lawman as altogether different. "I told you how close it came to being an armed attack on Bricker's ranch last night," he said. "What is there to hesitate about? If you're afraid of jumping in yourself, then send for the county sheriff . . . but don't just stand there."

He'd stung the lawman with those words and saw that he had when the deputy stumped back to his desk, dropped down, and swung around, his face red and his pale eyes like twin chips of ice.

"Fear's got nothing to do with it. Nothing at all to do with it."

"Then what has?"

The deputy fidgeted. He craned around Walt to gaze outward into the deserted, shimmering roadway. He brought his gaze back and swung it once around the room before turning back again to Walt. He said nothing for a while longer, not until he drifted his glance to a paper upon the desk and rapped it with a rough set of knuckles.

"This has," he finally growled, staring briefly at the paper before pushing it at Walt.

The paper was a resignation from office. Beneath its terse statement, giving age and infirmities as the reasons, was the signature of Fred Wheeler, Constable of Sunflower and Deputy Sheriff of Huachuca County.

Walt handed the paper back, stood a while gazing at Wheeler, and blew out a long breath. There was dogged indomitability in Wheeler's blunt jaw and bear-trap mouth. He and Walt stared back and forth for a moment of bleak silence.

"How long you been at it?" Walt asked, after several stretched out minutes.

"Twenty-seven years."

"Would another week make so much difference, Deputy?"

"It might, boy, it might. It'd make a lot of difference if Mike Weedon decided he didn't want to back off. Let me tell you something, Walt. A man gets to be my age . . . well, he gets almighty tired of making those long hard rides. But the prospect of steppin' in between two like Jim Bricker and Mike Weedon, well, now, that's a whole lot worse. Let the sheriff send a younger man down here for that one."

"Sure," said Walt in that dry tone of his, "and meanwhile the cussed roof falls in."

"Twenty-seven years, Walt, day and night, Saturday and Sunday, Christmas, New Year. . . . Need I go on?"

"Deputy, no man worth his salt steps out right when the things he believes in are endangered."

"What things, boy? I'm fifty-eight years old. I believe in roundin' out my life by dyin' in bed. That's what I believe in."

"Listen to me a minute. I'll do the riding, the hard work . . . you just back me up and give me the information I need."

Wheeler's testy eyes turned careful now. "What information? What backing up?"

"I can't say yet. I don't know. But I know this. There's got to be a way of stopping this thing. We both know how these things snowball. They start out on the range like a little bush fire, then, the first thing you know, they've taken in the town . . . hell, the whole county."

"Don't tell me about range wars," said the deputy wearily. "I've ridden into more of them than you've ridden into towns."

"Then you know what's likely to happen here. All I'm asking is for your cooperation. I'll take the chances, do the sweating and dodging."

Wheeler gazed steadily at Walt for a moment, then softly said: "Why? What's got you so fired up about this thing?"

"My folks died in a range war, Deputy. I've seen a few of them too. There's nothing that can ruin a country like one of those things . . . not even a dry summer or a winter with drifts of snow ten feet high. Folks forget bad times like dry summers, but they never forget dead friends. Never."

Fred Wheeler got up again. He paced up and down his little office. He made another smoke, popped it between his lips unlighted, and never did light it. He swung around near the cell-block door in the rear of the room and glared.

"You should've been a preacher," he snarled. "It's like hearin' cornhusks rattling dry and dusty in my memory, hearing you talk. Thirty years ago I was all fired up with the same kind of zeal, Walt. Right was always snow white and wrong was always dirty black. Well, it's never really like that at all. Take my word for it. There's a lot more gray in this lousy world than there is white *or* black, and that's a damned fact."

Wheeler resumed his pacing. He'd been stung somewhere on a raw nerve end. Walt knew this and waited. No more words were going to influence that flinty old man. He'd make this decision by himself.

Eventually he crossed to the desk, picked up that resignation, glowered at it, crumpled it in one oaken fist, and tossed it into a wastebasket.

"All right," he growled. "Put on your shining armor, Walt, and I'll show you just how wrong you are at the same time you're right." Wheeler looked ruefully at that crumpled paper in the wastebasket. "But there's one thing you've got to remember. I got no authority to appoint you a deputy sheriff or a deputy town constable, either. You're absolutely without authority and anything you do, you'll be doing on your own hook. Now you remember that."

Walt stepped back into the office, eased back down upon that wall bench, and inclined his head at the wrathful older man.

"I'll remember," Walt stated flatly. "Now then, tell me how you think we can get around Mike Weedon."

"We can't," stated Wheeler bluntly. "And furthermore, Jim Bricker doesn't have any patent on the north country. He's got prior rights, that's all, and in a showdown prior rights don't mean a blessed thing. Nearly every acre of this valley land is free graze. The cowmen generally own about half the land they run cattle on. So, if Mike decides he wants to drift cattle up where Jim's been running his critters all these years, there's legally not a cussed thing Jim can do about it." Wheeler paused, drew in a breath, and scowled. "Now," he growled, "you got any bright ideas how to get around that?"

"Talking to Weedon wouldn't make any difference?"

"No more than whistling in a wind storm, Walt."

"There's got to be some way though."

"There is. Leave 'em alone."

Walt shook his head. "You know better than that. It'll end up in a fight."

Wheeler leaned back in his chair. "I'll make you a bet!" he exclaimed. "It'll end up in a fight anyway, if it's got as far along as you say."

"Deputy, have a talk with them both."

"I aim to. I've aimed to ever since you came in here and started talkin', Walt. That's how you always start out. You have a talk with 'em. It never amounts to a damned thing, but that's how it has to start out . . . you have a lousy talk with them."

The deputy's bitterness almost infected Walt, but he resisted it. Wheeler sat across from him with his troubled stare, hard and disillusioned. He suddenly seemed to think of something because his lips softened and his expression turned quietly loose, eventually, and when Walt sat on with his private thoughts, saying nothing, the deputy slowly rocked forward in his chair to speak.

"It's Leila, isn't it?" he asked in a completely altered tone of voice. "Walt, it's Leila . . . that's why you're buyin' in, isn't it."

"You're good at guessing, Deputy Wheeler. It's Leila."

Wheeler leaned back in his chair again. This time he lifted both booted feet, slung them upon his desk top, and swiveled around just enough to see out. In a soft, even voice he said: "Just like thirty years ago . . . even to the girl with the honey-colored hair and the winter-day way of looking at a man. It makes me feel kind of uneasy, boy. It's too much like time was running in reverse for me."

Walt stood up. "I'm going to dust it out of town until nightfall," he said. "Weedon's crew knows me. They've got reason to push for a fight, too.

70

That would upset things before we even get started. See you later."

"Sure," murmured the deputy, without looking around at Walt or moving from where he sat. He sat, staring at nothing in particular as he mumbled: "See you later, after dark. Just like time was running in reverse for me. . . ."

Walt passed on out of the lawman's office, cut through to the rearward alley, and went up to the livery barn for his horse. He had another reason for wanting to be alone. He had to devise some way to stop a range war. The best place for that kind of concentration, he thought now, was back up there by the secret spring.

CHAPTER SEVEN

But Walt never got back to the secret spring. He was heading that way, was in fact a couple of miles north of Sunflower when the solid sound of gunshots scattered his thoughts, turning him instantly alert and wary.

It was dusk now, with evening's first long shadows settling in over the land from the roundabout peaks and slopes. Visibility was limited but sounds carried well in the cooling quiet. At first he thought that the gunfire had come from the north, but then when it erupted again after a little interval it seemed to come on from the west.

It didn't occur to Walt right away that this was a running fight, but when it did, he stopped dead still, sensing peril. The third time those ragged shots broke out he placed them easily because they were rapidly descending from the northward straight down toward him.

He reined off finally, spurred clear as the initial roll of a running horse came to him. For a moment there was no more shooting so he concentrated upon just listening.

It struck him that one man was fleeing wildly southward and that two or three other men were pursuing him. He had no idea who the fleeing man was nor, for that matter, who his pursuers were, but in the light of what he already knew about the trouble in the north country, he made a hasty deduction and came up with as incorrect a synopsis about this running fight as Fred Wheeler had come up with back in Sunflower about Walt himself.

He thought some B-Back-to-Back riders had caught a Weedon man upon their north country range. And he thought this right up to the revealing moment that a sagging man went lurching past eastward without seeing Walt, without even looking around. That man was B-Back-to-Back's range boss, Carl, and he'd been hit. He was riding loose and hanging on with both hands, his head lolling, his wiry body barely staying atop his frightened horse.

For a second, Walt stared. He had no reason to feel anything for Carl, but the odds here were a little more than he'd have felt like condoning, regardless, so he jumped out his horse to land between the wounded man and those pounding riders pushing along after him.

For a long second he had time to think, to wonder what had happened, then they came out of the night, like shadows in a rush at him. He raised his six-gun, fired once over their heads, lowered the gun, and snapped off two more shots. The foremost cowboy let off a loud cry and yanked back. He'd been hit and showed it the way he flung around in the saddle.

The other two riders were too surprised at Walt's abrupt appearance and unmoving stance to do more than fling a wild shot apiece, then fight their excited horses around. He did not fire at either of those two, but waited out the scrambled moments while they got the wounded man's horse between them and went racing westerly out into the deepening dark.

He swung to go after Carl, looped his reins upon the horn, and reloaded as he ran along. He had to halt twice to listen before he caught up with B-Back-to-Back's range boss, for although Carl was shot through he did not fall from his saddle or slow his horse. The animal eventually lost enough of its panic to heed its own exhaustion. It was slowing, jolting along in a straight course for Sunflower, when Walt overtook it, leaned out to pull back on a flopping rein, and halt the horse.

He swung down, stepped over and caught Carl as the dark, wiry man began to list off to one side. He had the full burden of the range boss to support for a moment before he could lower him. He was surprised at Carl's lightness; he didn't seem to weigh more than a hundred and fifty pounds.

The horses stood there blowing, coming back down to normalcy after their excitement, as Walt eased the injured man flat out on a matting of tough, short grass. He peered close for Carl's injury, saw how a bullet had struck him low in the back, gone through, and emerged out front not more than six inches above his belt buckle. It was a bad wound, not the kind that hurt a man too much, but the kind that for all its numbing effect, could very easily be fatal.

Carl drifted back and forth between consciousness and unconsciousness. In one lucid moment he recognized the man kneeling there beside him and said in a normal enough voice: "Well, you got it done, didn't you?"

Walt shook his head. "It wasn't me," he said. "It was Weedon's crew. I shot one of them and recognized the stocky one they call George."

"George Finster," said Carl. "Maybe you're tellin' the truth. Maybe you wasn't with 'em." He rolled his head around, looking back, and then on up at Walt again. "Where are they?"

"They left after I winged that one. What the devil started it?"

"I was headin' for the ranch, saw some men pushin' a bunch of cattle up from the south, and rode down there." Carl winced, ground his teeth, very gingerly eased off the tension, and went on: "They saw me comin' and split up. Reckon I should've known, but I didn't figure much about it. They got on my left and on my right. Then the one out front yelled for me to beat it . . . to go on away. I stopped to call back. I cussed that fellow.

He was a long way off, but his critters weren't and they were wearin' Weedon's marks. The one off on my right shot at me. I turned to shoot back and the one on my left let me have it. It felt like all the breath was being plumb knocked out of me. I turned and dug in the spurs. They took after me shootin' and runnin'. Reckon they had to finish the job so's I couldn't tell who done it."

Walt glanced again at that quietly spreading claret stain low on the prone man's body and said: "Care for a smoke, Carl?"

The dark man's lips puckered into an attempt at a little bleak smile. "I'd like that, sure. Tell me somethin', Hodge. Leila thinks you're all right. I don't. I told her pa you're a Weedon man sure. Now tell me right out . . . are you or aren't you?"

"Right out, Carl . . . no, I'm not. Like I told Leila, I'm no one's man."

"All right, I believe you. Why did you run them fellows off then? You favor B-Back-to-Back?"

"I've got no hand in this fight, Carl. Well, not the way you're thinking I might have, anyway. As for the others . . . I just didn't like the odds. Three to one, and you gut-shot."

"Ahh?" groaned the range boss. "Gut-shot?"

Walt went to work making the smoke. After he'd lit the thing, he placed it between Carl's lips. He didn't reply until Carl asked again about his wound.

"Is it the big one, Hodge?"

"I don't know about that, Carl, but I'll tell you this, you're not going to any dances for a while."

Walt eased back as though to stand up.

Carl's dark eyes jumped to Walt's face instantly; there was something close to fear in them. "Don't go," he said, his words beginning to drag a little, to thicken and turn deeply resonant.

"I got to go, Carl. I got to round up some help for you. You're bleeding inside and that's got to be stopped."

"I can read in your face what you're thinkin', Hodge, and if you're right . . . Hell . . . it's a long ride to town. You'd never find the sawbones and get back here in time."

"I figured to head for B-Back-to-Back."

"You better not. They'll shoot you on sight regardless of what Leila's been sayin'. Just set here with me a little longer."

Walt looked up and around. There was something like shock waves in the air. Something like the turmoil which preceded sound just before it was audible.

"Damned smoke went out," muttered Carl peevishly and drowsily. "Hodge?"

"Yeah."

"She gave me hell all the way home for crackin' you in the jaw."

"We're even about that, Carl."

Those dark eyes seemed to be turning dry, turning degrees cooler than was normal, but they vaguely smiled upward in their cloudy way.

"Yeah, we're even. Boy, you sure clouted me. Figured my jaw was busted."

"Leila said it was cracked. That's what she told me this morning."

"Naw. But I didn't know it wasn't until this afternoon when I ate a damned apple. You got a good punch."

"You too, Carl."

"No hard feelings?"

"No. Listen, you've got to have help. Suppose I fire off a couple of rounds. Maybe they'll hear 'em at the ranch."

"They should've heard them other shots," said Carl. "I was closer to the home place then, than we now are. They probably did and will be comin' along about now." This seemed to jar the range boss back to his former sharpness. He spat out the dead smoke and looked up with a little frown. "Don't let 'em catch you here. Like I said, Jim and the others figure you're one of Weedon's men. They catch you like this . . . well, I don't think you'd stand a chance."

"I'll listen," said Walt. "Carl, you think I ought to stay, so I'm going to tell you something. That's a right bad-looking wound you've got."

"Oh hell, I know that. You don't have to baby me none, Hodge. This is it. This is the big one. I thought so when the damned thing hit me. Only I wanted to get home before I croaked and let 'em know who was responsible."

"You said you didn't recognize them. You said they were too far off."

"But I sure enough recognized Weedon's cattle."

Walt suddenly lifted his head. Some distance off and rushing along north-easterly was a hurrying band of riders. He gauged their route and numbers. Carl also heard that drum-roll thunder.

He made a weak little gesture with one hand and said: "It'll be Jim and the boys. They heard the fight. Hodge, you better drift. Don't let 'em catch you."

Walt stood up, gazed a moment longer at Carl, then drew out his six-gun, lifted it, and fired one shot. "That'll let 'em know where you are," he told Carl. "Good luck."

"Thanks."

"And don't worry about the fellows who did this. I recognized one of 'em. I promise you, I'll find the others too." Then Walt stepped away and turned to go to his horse.

Carl's head rolled. He took a big breath and raggedly let it out. "Leila's a good judge of men," he said drowsily. "Treat her good, Hodge. She's all wool and a yard wide."

Walt settled across his saddle, listened a moment to that oncoming body of riders in the moonless night, called downward: "I'll treat her good! So long!"

With one last look back, he reined off eastward so as to be well out of the way of the approaching B-Back-to-Back men when they came down-country and found their dying range boss.

All this hadn't taken as long as Walt thought, for as he solemnly gazed southward he could faintly detect a skiff of paleness off across the far-away sky as though somewhere down there total night had not yet engulfed the world.

He rode eastward for a while, passing along slowly, before he swung southward and rode straight for Sunflower.

Whatever his reluctant ally Fred Wheeler had thought before, he now was going to have the solidest of reasons for altering those thoughts. Walt did not know Jim Bricker, had in fact never seen him so far as he knew, and yet he was familiar with Bricker's type. No one murdered the foreman of a big cow outfit in Arizona or anywhere else west of the muddy Missouri, without causing guns to be oiled and loaded up so that other men might get astride and go in search of trouble.

He came within sight of Sunflower, still thinking somber thoughts, and halted out there in the lonely night to wonder whether or not Mike

Weedon yet knew what had happened this night on the B-Back-to-Back range.

Walt figured if Weedon did know, he might not stay in town. Most likely he'd head for wherever he ordinarily made his plans and did his thinking, which would more than likely be his home ranch somewhere south of Sunflower.

Still, Walt had no intention of riding in and stumbling upon any of Weedon's men, in case his judgment was incorrect, so he eased out around the town, came into its westerly byways with distant music coming to him from along Main Street somewhere, and hid his horse as he'd done once earlier, before proceeding on foot to the lawman's shabby little combination office and jailhouse.

He made it, encountered no one up close, although the night's coolness after the daytime sun blast had brought forth a good many strollers.

Inside Wheeler's office, the deputy was shaving over at a little washstand. He glanced ahead into his fly-specked mirror, paused only for the space of one razor stroke as he recognized Walt standing across the room behind him, then went on shaving.

"Been wonderin' when you'd show up," the lawman said casually, made another long sweep with the razor, dipped it in a wash basin, lifted it for another stroke, and then riveted his attention upon Walt's face before slowly turning around.

"You look a little peaked," Wheeler said.

"I got reason to, Deputy. Weedon's men just shot Bricker's range boss. I was with him out there on the range just before I rode on down here."

Deputy Wheeler seemed to have forgotten the razor he was holding up. He stared over at Walt. In a voice almost gentle it was so soft, he said: "Kill him?"

Walt's answer was slow and dragging. "By now he'll be dead, Deputy. Shot him right through the soft parts. He was dying when I left him."

"You sure about it bein' Weedon's men?"

"I recognized the one named George Finster."

"Oh Lord," mumbled Fred Wheeler. "Oh Lord."

CHAPTER EIGHT

Deputy Wheeler turned back and mechanically finished shaving. He didn't say another word for as long as this took him. Even afterward, as he was cleaning his razor and putting away the shaving mug, dragging a towel over his face and neck, he said nothing. But when he'd completed his work and crossed over toward his desk, he said: "Tell me about it."

Walt related what he knew in a dispassionate way, watching for Wheeler's reaction. When he'd said all there was to tell, he went over to the wall bench and dropped down.

Wheeler shook his head. "I knew Carl," he said. "Knew his father and his mother. She was mostly Injun, but she sure was a fine woman. His father . . . well, he wasn't exactly my kind of a man, but I guess in his way he was all right." Wheeler went on, shaking his head. "I've known Carl since he was a kid. Rough, tough, sometimes a little meaner than a man ought to be, but one thing you could sure say for him. He'd have laid down and died for the Brickers."

"That's exactly what he did tonight," murmured Walt. "But that's over and done with, Deputy."

Wheeler looked over and gravely inclined his head. "I know," he muttered. "I know what you're thinkin'. Well, go on and crow if you want to. Being right gives a man that privilege."

"Crow hell," growled Walt. "Like I told you before . . . I want to see this thing stopped before it gets any worse."

"Hah!" snorted Fred Wheeler. "It won't be stopped now, boy. No one shoots one of Jim Bricker's men and gets away with it. Earlier I told you about Mike Weedon. Well, let me give you a little sketch about Jim. He's red-headed and red-necked and has a temper of fire. He didn't put together his B-Back-to-Back outfit by being like a Sunday schoolteacher. He's got a lot more tolerant these past ten years or so, but he's still no man to push around. And one other thing too. Jim Bricker took Carl on as a troublesome young cowboy, knocked some sense into him, learnt him about responsibility, about the ranching business . . . and no one's going to kill Carl and not have Jim to fight. No one at all, and you can believe that, Walt."

All the time he'd been speaking, Wheeler had been buckling on his shell belt. Once he finished this, he looked up. There was that tough-set look to his features Walt had seen earlier this same day.

"What're you going to do?" Walt asked.

"Not me," replied the deputy sheriff. "*Us*. You said you recognized George Finster. All right. Now the two of us are going down to Weedon's place, where you're going to have another look, make plumb sure it was George you saw, then we're going to arrest him and fetch him back here to jail."

Walt stood up. "It was George. I told you he was at the Variety House yesterday with Weedon and those others. I don't need any second look. I'd swear it was George on a stack of Bibles. And, Deputy, get Weedon to trot out his other men as well . . . one of 'em's packing a slug from my gun. I know I winged him when I interfered with the killing of Bricker's range boss."

Now Deputy Wheeler settled in his boots over there by the desk and gazed upon Walt with a changing look. "You afraid to ride out there with me?" he quietly asked.

Walt returned that look. "Afraid hell," he said tartly. "Weedon doesn't scare me worth a damn."

"Then you'll come with me?"

"No. I'm going up to B-Back-to-Back and stop Bricker from starting anything before he gets under way."

Wheeler considered this for a moment. It made sense to him even though his doubting look said plainly enough he doubted that Walt could accomplish it. He had his mouth open to speak, to say something relevant, when out in the roadway a number of riders came up and halted, their rein chains, saddles, and fidgeting shod horses making an unmistakable sound in the night.

Very slowly Wheeler looked over at his door. Walt also looked, wondering who would come inside through that panel. He didn't have long to wait and although he'd never seen this man before, he recognized him on sight. It was Jim Bricker. He was as Wheeler had told Walt before, a red-headed, powerfully built man with a flash of temper to his willful gaze.

Bricker entered the deputy's office alone. He stopped after giving the door a slam, spread his thick legs, and looked from Wheeler to Walt, then back to Wheeler again. There was death in his face as plain as day.

He said: "Fred, Carl's outside. He's tied face down over his saddle."

Wheeler nodded gently. "I know," he murmured.

"You know?" said Jim Bricker. "How do you know? It only happened an hour or so ago."

"Jim, this here young fellow is Walt Hodge. He was with Carl right after your man got shot."

Bricker's head whipped around. His lips flattened and for just a second Walt thought Bricker might spring at him.

"You're Hodge, are you?" ground out the cowman. "I want you bad, cowboy. I want you for the killing of my range boss!"

"What!" Walt exclaimed, nonplussed by this totally unexpected charge.

"You heard me. We found your tracks, Hodge. It took a lot of doing but we followed 'em down here to town."

"Bricker," said Walt, recovering from the shock slowly, "I'm the one who fired off that shot to let you know where Carl was. He was alive then. In fact it was Carl who told me to clear out before you got there."

"Yeah," growled the bleak-faced cattleman. "Say anything you want because you know damned well Carl can't call you a liar. Fred, I want this man arrested for murder."

Wheeler, listening to all this, seemed no less surprised than Walt had been. He didn't say anything though. For a long time, he simply kept staring over at Walt.

"Fred! You deaf or something? I said this man . . ."

"I heard you, Jim," the lawman growled, interrupting Bricker. "All right, I'll arrest him. But I'm a long way from being convinced he shot Carl." Wheeler strolled closer to Bricker and Walt could find no trace of trepidation at all in the lawman's face as he halted five feet off and, giving Bricker look for look, said roughly: "Was Carl dead when you got up to him with your crew?"

"Of course he was dead. Shot from the back plumb through."

"Was he still warm and limp, Jim?"

87

"Yes, he couldn't have been dead more than perhaps a couple of minutes."

"Then I think what Hodge has told me Carl said before he died is the truth."

"What do you mean?" demanded Bricker. "Whatever this damned murderer told you is a . . ."

"Hold on, Jim. You're fired up. I understand why that is, but just because you're mad doesn't mean I'm going to charge Hodge with murder. I want some answers to other things first."

Bricker glared. He stiffened there by the door, looking savage and near to violence. But in the face of this, Fred Wheeler's expression did not change at all. In Walt's view it was fire burning against granite.

"Go on now, Jim," said Wheeler in that same roughened tone. "Take Carl over to the embalming shed and then take your men on back to the ranch. I'll lock Hodge up. This thing's going to be handled legal-like."

Bricker slowly turned and Walt had to brace into his savage fury. He glared for a long time. For a while it seemed that he would hurl harsh words at Walt, but in the end he simply turned, opened the door, passed on out into the night, and slammed the door behind himself with such force the entire jailhouse reverberated. Not until he was finally gone did Walt loosen his body.

Deputy Wheeler looked him up and down

before he said, "I'm not locking you up on his say-so, Walt. I'm locking you up because you're the only witness to a murder so far, and if I don't, the minute you step outside this building someone's going to cut you down sure as the devil." Wheeler went over and held out a hand for Walt's six-gun. He shrugged as he did this and said: "Call it protective custody if you like, or maybe just life insurance, but I'll be gone maybe two, three hours over at Weedon's place. I want to be blessed sure you'll be alive and handy when I get back."

Walt lifted out his gun, placed it gently upon Wheeler's outstretched palm, pushed back his hat, and let off a long exhalation.

"I never thought for a moment this thing could take a turn like it has. I thought sure Carl would live long enough to tell Bricker what he also told me."

"Maybe he was leaking blood internally faster than you thought he was," muttered Wheeler, returning to his desk. He dropped Walt's gun over there, scooped up a large brass key ring, and started toward that yonder cell-block door. "Come along. Let's get this over with. I got a heap of riding to do between now and tomorrow morning."

As Walt preceded the lawman through that door and toward one of the strap-steel cages beyond, where it was dingily dark and moldy smelling,

Wheeler said: "I thought you agreed to do all the ridin' and rushin' around in this mess."

As Walt turned, letting Wheeler pass by to open the locked cell door, he saw that the lawman was mirthlessly smiling at his own small joke.

"Which one of us do you believe?" Walt said, letting that feeble bit of humor go past.

Wheeler flung back the door and replied as Walt stepped through. "You. But even if I didn't, I'd still favor waiting a few days until Bricker calms down. You know, for a moment there I thought he might draw on you."

"Me too. So, Deputy, thanks for believing. It's all the truth, exactly as I told you."

Wheeler clanged the door closed, locked it, hooked his key ring over his holstered six-gun, and made a wry face. "I got to believe you, Walt. There's nothin' else to go on right now. But let me warn you . . . if George Finster's got a good alibi for his whereabouts tonight, and if I don't find a wounded man down at the Weedon Ranch . . . well . . . you're in serious trouble. Real serious."

Walt stood there gazing out. It occurred to him that if Wheeler came back empty-handed from the Weedon place, the law still couldn't prove he'd shot Carl because there had been no actual witnesses to that shooting except the men involved, and there was no survivor either. Then, to shatter this illusion, came a second notion, and this one held him stone still. Weedon's killers could swear under oath they'd seen Walt kill Carl!

"You don't look so good," muttered Wheeler from out in the gloomy little passageway. "Don't sweat too much. If you didn't do it, I'll find out."

"Deputy?"

"Yeah."

"Suppose Finster and those other two say *I* shot Carl."

Wheeler's expression didn't alter. "That's already occurred to me," he said. "It would be tough refuting a charge like that, especially when there were three of them and one of you . . . and you're a total stranger hereabouts. But, while men can lie themselves out of a lot of things, tell me something. How does a shot man lie himself out of being shot?"

"By saying it was an accident!" exclaimed Walt quickly.

"Depends," countered the lawman. "Depends on where the bullet hit him, and which man he is, and some other things like where he was when he got it and who was there with him. Mainly though, Walt, it depends on just how far those others will go in lying for Mike Weedon, if Mike set those fellows to kill Carl."

Wheeler unhooked the key ring from over his six-gun, twirled it thoughtfully for a moment, then nodded and walked away. Walt heard him pass on out into his office but beyond that he heard nothing because the oaken panel separating his cell-block from Wheeler's outer room was not only iron bound, it was also indestructibly thick. He paced once the length of his small cell, once the width of it, halted over where the back wall loomed darkly windowless, made a smoke, and lit it.

He had counted on Carl living long enough to explain to Bricker what had really happened. Now it appeared that Carl knew he was failing faster than Walt had thought he was. It had never once crossed his mind that he would be catapulted into the position of an accused murderer and this idea now took a little getting used to. He finished the cigarette, tried to estimate the time, thought it could be no later than perhaps ten o'clock, wondered how long it would take Wheeler to see Weedon and return, crossed to the chained-up wall bunk, and perched upon the edge of it.

It occurred to him after a while that he was still, although now in a totally unexpected manner, keeping Bricker and Weedon apart in their snow-balling feud. It also occurred to him that as long as he remained helplessly locked up, this condition could change at any moment. Fred Wheeler, for all his knowledge of those two antagonists, and despite his twenty-seven years' experience as a lawman, was still just one man. He could be expected to do the routine thing, but

Walt was sure the routine thing was not going to be enough.

The longer he sat there in his world of gloomy silence, the more restless he became. He hadn't had much rest these last twenty-four hours and should have been sleepy now, but he'd never been more fully awake in his lifetime.

CHAPTER NINE

Deputy Wheeler was gone much longer than Walt had anticipated. In fact he didn't return until dawn was making its pale, pale glow off in the distant east, and Walt heard him at the cell-block door only moments after he'd heard the roadside door open and close.

He got up, wanting to see who Wheeler had brought back with him from Weedon's ranch.

Wheeler came through that oaken door all by himself. He walked calmly down and halted to peer in at Walt.

"Where's Finster?" asked Walt.

Wheeler said tiredly: "Out at the ranch. I didn't bring him in."

"You what? You know he's the key to that murder. If he leaves the country . . ."

"Whoa," interrupted Wheeler. "Just listen for a minute. I didn't accuse George of anything and I didn't say why I wanted to talk to Mike Weedon. They were all there and they were wondering so bad about why I'd ridden in to see the bunch of 'em it was like signs on their faces, but I didn't say anything and they were afraid to ask."

"What the hell kind of nonsense is this?" Walt demanded.

"I'm trying to tell you. On the way out there,

94

I got to thinking. Listen now. Jim Bricker's convinced you shot Carl. He cut your sign and somehow figured out it was your horse he and his crew trailed into Sunflower. I don't know exactly how he did that, but I can guess some mark or other on your horse's shoes. But that's not important right now. What *is* important is that Jim thinks you're the killer . . . not Weedon's bunch. You see what I'm driving at?"

"I see. As long as Bricker figures I'm the killer, he won't go after Weedon."

"Right. Now Finster and whoever was with him tonight knows who killed Carl. Maybe they told Mike and maybe they didn't. But regardless of that, Mike told me he was coming to town tomorrow."

"Well, what of it?"

"I'm going to arrest Finster, Charley Murchison, and Les Upton."

Wheeler let this last statement hang there for a moment, let it hang there long enough for Walt to start a faint, uncomprehending scowl.

Wheeler didn't add anything for at least a minute, then he said: "Les Upton has a bandaged right hand. He says he hurt it building a fence at the ranch. I don't think so. I think he's got a bullet hole through it, and that it was him that you heard cry out when you fired off those shots." Wheeler paused again. He smiled thinly and said softly: "Remember what I told you . . . that it all depends

95

where a man's wearing a bullet hole? Well, Walt, no right-handed man can very well shoot himself in the right hand while he's holding his own gun, so when Les comes to town tomorrow, I'm going to arrest him, have the sawbones waiting here at the jailhouse, strip off that bandage, and, for Les's sake, I sure hope he's got a barbed-wire cut instead of a bullet hole."

Walt ran this through his mind. He knew it was sound logic. He said: "All right, but what about those other two . . . Charley and George Finster?"

"I put my horse in Mike's barn instead of tying him over at the horse rack. I told Mike he needed a bait of feed, but I had a chance to look around a little."

"I see. So you found three ridden-down horses."

Wheeler shook his head. "Nope. They weren't that careless. There wasn't a horse in the barn or in the outside corrals, either."

"Then what?"

"Charley's saddle and George's saddle . . . they both had wet horse sweat on the sheep pelt under the skirts. Not another saddle hangin' there was still wet from a horse's back."

Walt looked out at Wheeler. Smiling, he said: "Twenty-seven years teaches a man a lot of tricks, doesn't it?"

The deputy smiled. "The best trick it teaches a fellow is to stay alive. I'm not sure yet whether Mike's in this killin' or not, but I do know the minute I make those arrests he's going to explode. All I got to figure out between now and the time he rides into Sunflower with his men, is how to use a trick or two to keep from gettin' blown apart."

"Are you pretty sure he'll fight those arrests?"

"Sure as I can be. Mike Weedon's like Jim Bricker in one way. You tangle with one of his men and you'll have Mike to fight as well."

"But not the law . . . he wouldn't . . ."

"Walt, you've got a lot to learn about these Arizonans. They'll fight the law sometimes quicker than they'll fight one another. If Mike has his way, he'll turn my town into a battleground. I know him and I know his type. Mike Weedon will fight, so will his other men."

"Arm a bunch of the townsmen," Walt suggested.

"They'd laugh me off the streets if I went to them before Mike even rode in, but that doesn't worry me. What does, though, is the simple fact that as soon as the hangers-on over at Mike's favorite bar, the Variety House, got wind of what I was preparin' for him when he rode in with his men, Mike wouldn't come, or else he'd come shootin'. Those hangers-on over there wouldn't waste a minute rushin' to Mike's ranch to warn him."

Walt had evidently been thinking ahead of the deputy because Wheeler had no sooner finished speaking than he said: "All right, then I'll escape. I'll bust out of your jail."

The lawman's bushy brows climbed, but he asked no questions. He simply stood out there waiting.

"I'll bust out and you'll form a posse among the townsmen. That way you'll have a big armed crowd behind you when Weedon's crew rides into town. No one will know in advance what you plan to do because even Weedon's friends here in Sunflower will think you're making your posse to go after me . . . and then you make your arrests."

Wheeler kept staring in at Walt for as long as it took for this scheme to resolve itself favorably or unfavorably in his mind. He slowly smiled and inclined his head.

"It's pretty good," he ultimately said. "I'd have thought of it myself, I reckon, in time."

"Sure you would have," chuckled Walt. "What time do you expect Weedon's crew?"

"Don't know, but he seldom ever rides in before ten, eleven in the morning." Wheeler pursed his lips, drew forth from a vest pocket a massive old gold watch. He flicked open its face cover, squinted at the spidery black hands, and replaced the thing as he said: "Hell, it's after my breakfast time already. It's nine o'clock."

"Unlock this door," said Walt, "and give me back my gun. I'll wait in the office until you fetch my horse." Walt explained where he'd left the animal the night before as Wheeler released him. Afterward, they both went out to the deputy's desk and Walt took up his gun, examined its loads, dropped the thing into his hip holster as he said: "On second thought, leave my horse at the livery barn to be grained and cared for, and fetch me back a fresh livery animal. If there's any running to be done, I want a fresh horse under me."

Thoughtfully, Wheeler reached up to scratch the tip of his nose. "It just came to me," he said slowly. "Why not just *say* you've escaped and let it go at that, while you stay locked up?"

"Someone is bound to check here. Anyway, it's going to look a lot more authentic if a few folks see me leaving town."

"Yeah," mumbled the lawman dourly. "But if one of those folks happens to up and shoot you . . . then what?"

"Not much chance, providing you fetch me back a good horse from the livery barn. Besides, I don't suppose too many even know who I am yet or what I've supposedly done."

"Hah," grunted the lawman. "Don't fool yourself on that score. Jim Bricker's boys will have hit the Dallas House a time or two since last night. They'll have told about Carl and about you. No doubt everybody in town will have heard the tale by this time."

"I'll have to take that chance, but you fetch me back a good horse."

Deputy Wheeler crossed over to the door but he began to look like a man with sudden and increasing doubts. Still, he departed, closed the door very carefully behind himself, and called back for Walt to bar it from the inside, then went stumping northward along the plank walk with his sturdy footfalls hollowly echoing.

Walt reconsidered his plan. He found it a long way from being foolproof, but he had a reason for wishing to be out of protective custody that he had not confided to Deputy Wheeler.

It had come to him while he and Wheeler had been talking in the cell-block that if B-Back-to-Back's range boss had died before Bricker and his men found him, then Carl would have had no chance to tell them Walt was not one of Weedon's men, as they all evidently thought, and this being so, then Bricker wouldn't be content to let things remain as they were because he'd believe Weedon was still responsible for the death of Carl. Bricker would not be content to let the law handle Carl's killing. He might be willing, in fact he seemed likely, to let the law have Walt who he thought was Carl's actual murderer. But Walt was willing to wager that Bricker was right this minute making plans to go after Weedon.

That was his private reason for wishing to be free. He had no idea how to accomplish it, but he knew that somehow he had to prevent Bricker from riding.

He had considered and discarded a dozen ideas before Wheeler returned with a stout buckskin horse, tied this saddled animal to his outside rack, crossed over, and rapped upon the door. Walt admitted him.

"He'll get you where you got to go," said the deputy, jerking a thumb over one shoulder. "And your horse is stalled at the barn." Wheeler hooked both thumbs in his shell belt, put his head a little to one side, and skeptically said: "This better work all around for both of us."

Walt pushed the door nearly closed. "Yeah," he assented in that dry tone of voice. "It sure better. Well, Deputy, you know any reason why I can't make it out of town?"

"No. Just walk out there, get astride, and walk your horse southward. Don't run and don't keep your hat back off from your face like it is now. Yank it low. No one's going to pay you any attention until I rush out of here hollerin' that you got away." Wheeler's expression turned dour. "I've never lost a prisoner in my life, so folks are goin' to start growlin' that I'm so old I let you escape. It's downright humiliatin', Walt."

"It won't be that way for long," Walt said, taking hold of the door's smooth edge. "I'll come back tonight, late."

Wheeler nodded. "Good luck," he murmured.

"And remember now . . . just ride casual out of town."

Walt opened the door, shot a look out, saw nothing to hold him back, and stepped down onto the plank walk. He knew Wheeler was watching him from inside the office. He got to the buckskin, unloosed the reins, checked the cincha, and stepped up to wheel off southerly. He tugged his hat brim down low and let the stocky horse go hiking along through the fiery sunlight that seared down across them both.

Around him Sunflower was quiet and lethargic. He saw people idling along here and there, mostly women with market baskets. He wondered a little about the time, thought perhaps Fred Wheeler would have to cut it a little fine in order to raise his armed posse before Weedon's bunch got to town, then he was down among the shacks and shanties at the lower end of town.

Here there were even fewer people visible but the slab-sided dogs came out to sniff and look and sometimes bristle at him, sometimes wag raffish tails. There were several children playing, too, but they scarcely cast him a glance.

Then he was completely clear of Sunflower. Behind him, as he twisted for a last look, the roadway, the plank walks, even the stores, were as heat-wilted and indifferent-seeming as ever. He permitted himself a little smile, reined off westerly, and settled to a long ride.

He understood the folly of attempting to approach B-Back-to-Back boldly and riding straight-up, so he went west from town for a mile then swung northward toward the Saginaws, unconsciously heading for the secret spring, as he considered the knotty problem of seeing Jim Bricker without being shot before he could speak.

The heat rolled up over him. It was near midday and even the cattle of this range country had long ago sought shaded places to drowse through the worst of it. Those onward hazed mountainsides wore a gelatin shimmer. Their peaks were almost entirely lost in the rising heat mists.

Southward and eastward the land was a blue blaze. Westward, a shimmering mirage falsely showed an alluring lake lined with poplars whose shade was the deepest, most inviting shade Walt had ever seen.

He thought that he should hate all this punishing heat but he also thought Bricker would not lead his men after the Weedon bunch until the day cooled off, so he stoically accepted the glittering, fierce light as a kind of ally. He headed straight for the spring, willing for a while at least to forget Bricker in order to assuage the thirst that kept increasing the longer he passed along under that terrible sun.

He got to the spring, into that sticky and resin-scented shade of the place, and dismounted.

The stocky buckskin horse was wringing wet with foam at shoulder and saddle skirt. Walt off-saddled, led the beast over, and, using his hat for a bucket, washed the grateful animal. After that, he tied him back where the shade was thickest and stripped off his shirt to wash himself as well. He made no attempt to shake off surplus water and its drying cooled him pleasantly.

CHAPTER TEN

Walt had a smoke and watched its little bluish plume stand straight up in the breathless air. He drank and sat a while before drinking again. As far as he could see in three directions, there was no movement. In the fourth direction, up that rearward granite bulwark, there was only the dancing sun blast.

He was confident Bricker would wait at least another hour before he led out southward with his avenging crew. He also hoped that when Bricker did that, he'd head for Weedon's ranch and not Sunflower.

He speculated on Fred Wheeler's chances for success down in town as well. Their plan seemed sound enough. Wheeler would undoubtedly take Weedon by surprise and make his three arrests. But after that, after Wheeler had made his play, the next move would be Mike Weedon's and Walt had only his one-time meeting with Weedon to base a conclusion upon. Still, he had not tagged Weedon as a fool. As a bitterly hard and fearless man, yes, but a fool, no. Stripped of half his crew Weedon wouldn't be foolish enough to try and brace the entire town of Sunflower.

Or would he?

He heard the buckskin squaring around behind

him and looked. The animal was standing completely still, gazing far out with his head up and his little ears stiffly forward. Walt followed out the horse's line of vision and sighted movement. It was a rider atop a slow-pacing horse. Both of them seemed to be marching along ten inches off the heat-whitened ground; they seemed to weave, to grow taller and shorter, to go back and to come on.

He wondered who that might be, and had made up his mind long before he caught the flash of hot light off honey-blonde hair. Leila Bricker had her course set for the pine grove, which gave Walt enough time to put his shirt back on and walk to the outer limits of his quiet place to greet her. She saw him there. He sighted the quick lift of her chin and the soft settling of her body as though in relief.

She came right up to him, didn't smile, stepped down, and led her animal into shade. "I don't think I ever hoped for anything so much before," she murmured, tossing aside her hat and lifting a solemn gaze to him. "My father said you were in jail. I was on my way there now. But . . ."—she paused—"something drew me here." She smiled. "And here you are."

"Yes, I was in jail, but Deputy Wheeler and I have come up with a plan. I rode out to try and stop your father from going after Weedon."

She stepped along to the side of a huge old

rough-barked tree and limply leaned upon it. She didn't look around when he came up behind her, but gazed gravely over the southward run of gritty land.

"I don't see how one man can do that," she murmured. She turned suddenly to face him, to look up into his face. "I was also heading into town to tell Deputy Wheeler that the crew is going to head for Sunflower."

"Sunflower?"

"Yes. They're going to demand that Deputy Wheeler go with them and arrest Weedon's whole crew for contributing to Carl's death."

He let off a quiet long sigh. "Weedon's in Sunflower by now, Leila. Wheeler's going to arrest three men for Carl's killing. I think, if your father can be kept out of there just until tomorrow, Wheeler will have the whole thing under control."

"They're going to ride as soon as the sun sets, Walt."

"All right," he muttered, before adding: "Then we've got to devise some way to change that."

"How?"

He made a thin smile at her. "That's what we're going to figure out right now."

He took her hand, led her to the cool ground at the spring, and when she sank down, he dropped down beside her.

She waited for him to say something. He saw

this, saw that she was anxious for him to come up with an idea that would prevent serious trouble. She had some kind of hope in him. It showed from her liquid soft eyes.

But he had no plan and shook his head to indicate that this was so, then afterward noticed the let-down of that hope in her gaze. He reached for one of her hands and held it.

"Before he died . . . before I left him . . . Carl told me to be kind to you. He said you tried to tell the others I wasn't one of Weedon's crew."

"Yes, I told my father that. But he said he didn't believe it. He said you'd killed Carl."

"Yeah. If he'd just looked around out there, after daylight came, he'd have found other tracks too." Thinking back to the wildness in Jim Bricker's face when they'd first met at Fred Wheeler's office, Walt thought something tart and uncharitable, but he didn't say it. He said instead: "That's why I was up here now. I figured to cool off a little, then try to see your father before he hit the trail."

"You mustn't try that," she said swiftly. "The whole crew is fired up against you."

"There are ways," he murmured, thinking of one of them. "This time of day even your riders wouldn't be on their toes. I think I could slip in and see your father without the others knowing, with a little help, Leila."

She squeezed his fingers with a sudden surge. "No. It would be too dangerous, and if you make one slip, they'd kill you without giving you a chance. You don't know how they feel. Not just about you, but about Mike Weedon too."

For a while he looked at the trodden grass. Eventually he raised his head and said: "All right. You'll do it then."

"Me? Do what, Walt?"

"They couldn't get to Sunflower without horses, could they? You go on back, turn loose their animals, and set them afoot."

He waited, watching her face closely for reaction. When it came he saw the doubt, the misgivings, and spoke again.

"You're the only one who could pull that off, Leila."

She said faintly: "It would change things at that, wouldn't it? But they'd go after them, Walt. It wouldn't hold them up for too long."

"It wouldn't have to, Leila. If they can just be kept out of Sunflower for the balance of this day, I think Wheeler and I can do the rest. In fact, I wouldn't be surprised if Wheeler already has Weedon's end of it under control." He didn't mention the posse down in town. He didn't think this was necessary or even pertinent.

She looked out through the westerly trees a moment, then nodded.

"All right, I'll do it, Walt. But in case they get

the horses caught again before nightfall . . . what should I do then?"

"Leave that to me," he said, thinking that if she could do her part, he could ride fast back to town and get Fred Wheeler with his posse to come back up north with him, throw out a cordon, cutting off Bricker's advance southward, and in this manner prevent fighting.

"You have a plan?"

He smiled at her. "A shaky one, but I believe if your part works, mine will too. Trying something is better than doing nothing." He got up.

She caught his fingers and pulled herself upright, landing close to him. She watched him. She waited for him to speak. He didn't say a word, he only looked down at her and she was round-shaped and solid in his sight with her heavy mouth lying gently relaxed in its fullness. Her breasts rose and softly fell to her shallow breathing. The magic of her closeness was urgent. It strained him forward.

"Leila . . . ," he said, and let it trail off without adding anything to it. He moved both hands and swayed her to him, watching as her eyes widened as his head came down, saw her lips tilt to meet his mouth, then, at the meeting of their mouths, he was abruptly thrown off balance by a rush of his pent-up hungers. His desires rushed over them both, turning a gentle kiss to a demanding, bruising one.

For a moment she was rigid, but only for a moment. Her own fire came up to burn against him. There was something bitter in this abandon, something shameless and insistent as though, although she knew better, she did not wish to.

They parted, he stepping back one foot, she holding herself erect and still. She whispered: "You're thinking it was too easy, aren't you?"

He didn't answer. Instead he half turned her so filtered sunlight struck down across her face and throat. There was a tawny glow in her eyes that the sunlight heightened. It sang over to him, went down deep. He turned her back.

"It should've been easy," he murmured. "It should be like that when love comes to people. Knowing right off that this is *the* person you've been wandering through life looking for."

Her eyes turned misty toward him. Her lips licked at their outer corners. She put forth a hand to let it lie palm-forward upon his chest. "You make it sound right, Walt."

"It's been right since the first time I saw you. It couldn't be any other way than right, no matter what."

"You feel that, Walt?"

"More than that. Don't you?"

"Yes," she said. Her hand fell away. "Carl knew it. After he'd hit you and we were riding home, he kept watching me when I was angry because of what he did. He said we should take the long

111

way home . . . and we did. He told me while we were riding along that love came to people and made them act the way I was acting toward him." She looked outward beyond the trees, sobering as she recalled this thing she was relating. "I was indignant but he wouldn't say he could be wrong. That's how we rode home . . . me angry, Carl going along looking solemn and I think a little hurt." Her gaze came back to his face. "That's why he asked you to be kind to me. He knew."

Walt nodded. He was remembering Carl also. The things he'd said as he'd been dying in the cooling night. The way he'd looked up into Walt's face. Carl had known.

"How many times in his lifetime does a man think of love," he said to her. "Wondering when it's going to come and what she will be like. Then it comes and despite all that, he's entirely unprepared. I thought you were beautiful that first time, Leila, but with everything else crowding up, I didn't know this was the place and the time and the girl."

"I didn't either," she said, faintly frowning before shaking her head. "Or did I?"

He smiled at her. "I sure know it now."

She touched him, went up against him, and pushed her face into his chest. They stood like this for a long time before she straightened back again, her eyes sometimes a mist, sometimes a flame, rummaging his features as though to indelibly imprint them upon her heart.

"I don't want anything to happen to you, Walt. I'm afraid that after we leave here and are apart, something might happen. I don't want to leave here, Walt."

He touched her lightly, tenderly. His eyes were shaded to her as he partially turned to see their horses, and quite suddenly his hand upon her hardened, turned roughly sharp in its touch. She came jarring back down to normalcy by the swift change in him and parted her lips to speak, but instead she also turned a little to look beyond.

There was a cowboy out there, less than five hundred feet away, and coming steadily toward their secret place!

"It's Foster," she gasped. "Foster Babcock."

"A Bricker man?" he asked quickly, dropping his hand, turning fully to face that unsuspecting man out in the lemon-yellow heat waves.

"Yes. I thought he was at the ranch."

"Maybe he followed you."

"No . . . he wouldn't. What for?"

Walt shrugged, stepped away, and walked ahead where that drowsy-looking rider would enter the shaded place. It was clear that Foster Babcock had no idea he had caused any sudden turmoil on ahead. It was also obvious that nothing was at this moment farther from his thoughts than meeting another human being. He was riding as a man rides who is heat-whipped, thirsty, and completely resigned. His horse came slogging along, reins swinging, head down, eyes near closed. There was no alertness or awareness about either of them as they passed into the shade initially, saw Walt standing there, and halted dumbly to consider this totally unexpected phenomenon.

Foster Babcock was young, younger than Walt was by perhaps five or six years. He was an average-looking cowboy except for a sprinkling of freckles across the saddle of his nose and the formidable squareness of his heavy jaw. He sat upon his horse, looking and blinking for almost thirty seconds, before he moved at all or spoke.

"You're that fellow they call Hodge," Babcock said quietly, with no immediate apparent antagonism, or, for that matter, no immediate apparent understanding or comprehension.

Walt said: "Get down and keep that hand clear of your gun."

Babcock slowly obeyed, stepped up to his animal's head, and began to scowl. "I thought you was in jail. We heard over at the ranch you was . . ." Babcock's voice trailed off into deep silence. He was looking a little to his right where Leila had stepped forward out of the gloomy shadows. His mouth shot open, his jaw slack.

"Miss Leila . . . ?"

"Hello, Foster."

Babcock looked at Walt again. He was now thoroughly and obviously perplexed.

"How did you happen to come out here?" Leila asked.

The young cowboy answered candidly, still shocked at the sight of Leila. "Was out lookin' for sign of riders. Your pa sent me to do that. Got dry . . . so I headed for the spring. That's all, Miss Leila."

Leila looked over at Walt. "Now what do we do?" she asked.

"Tie him to a tree," said Walt, having already come to the conclusion that they could not risk letting Babcock ride off.

Leila nodded. She turned, saying: "You heard, Foster. I'm sorry. If it wasn't absolutely necessary, we wouldn't do that. I want you to believe me."

"Miss Leila," said the bewildered range rider, "I plumb don't understand. Your pa will have a fit if he knows you and this here Hodge fellow are seein' one another. Ma'am, Carl's hardly cold in his grave and you're flouncin' 'round with the fellow as shot him."

Walt went to Babcock's saddle, took down the lariat there, crossed over, and handed it to Leila. He stepped away dropping his right hand to his gun butt.

Leila looked at the rope, at Walt, then over at Babcock.

The cowboy's astonishment was dimming. He began to carefully appraise Walt, and Walt's right hand. There was no mistaking what was running through the rider's mind now.

Walt gently wagged his head. "Don't try it," he murmured. "You'd never make it, Babcock." Turning, he said to Leila: "Do your best. I'll check the knots after you're done. All right, Babcock, up against the tree behind you, and no cussin'."

Babcock went to the tree, his face slowly turning crimson. Leila tied him there. Walt checked the bonds, found them satisfactory, then said to the young woman: "Take his horse back with you. Turn it loose with the others. I'll stay here until you're gone."

She nodded, teetered a moment, then walked over, boldly stood up to her full height, kissed Walt squarely on the lips, turned, and without a glance at the tied man, whose cloudy eyes followed her with shock and amazement, went over, and mounted up. She said nothing, only caught the reins of Babcock's animal and rode on out of the shady place.

Walt watched her for a long time before he turned back toward the B-Back-to-Back man. Those two exchanged a long look. After several minutes Babcock said indignantly: "Her pa will kill you sure, Hodge, for what you've done to her."

"Done? What have I done?"

"You done romanced her and now she's all mixed up and helpin' the killer of her own range boss. That's what you've went and done."

"Foster, I didn't kill Carl. I haven't killed anyone around here. I'd hate like hell to have to start with you, so just stay tied here until one of us comes back and turns you loose."

"You won't get away with it, Hodge. Jim Bricker is the type of man who'll notice I'm still gone and he'll wonder about me."

"Yeah," muttered Walt in that dry tone as he headed for his horse. "All the same . . . maybe we did you a favor. If Bricker rides into Sunflower, you might be lucky you're not with him."

Then Walt mounted, nodded at Babcock, and also rode away.

CHAPTER ELEVEN

The resting tide of mid-day heat bore down with solid force as Walt went back down-country the same way he'd earlier ridden northward. He could not entirely ignore that heat, but he did the next best thing. He ran a number of related thoughts together in his head to weave a loose kind of continuity. If Leila succeeded in putting the B-Back-to-Back men on foot, and if he could get Fred Wheeler with his posse to ride out with him, then all could still end well.

Furthermore, there seemed no more likely person to do what Leila would seek to accomplish than Jim Bricker's own daughter. He wondered about the recriminations she would afterward harvest from her fiery father and his riders. It made him wince, thinking of that. And yet, even now with no disturbing influence to color his thinking, Walt remained convinced that their scheme was the best, under these circumstances.

The alternative of course had been for Leila to arrange a meeting between Walt and her father. But this idea had nearly as many obvious perils as possible benefits, so in the end, since he dared not seek out Bricker yet, putting the B-Back-to-Back afoot was the best strategy.

He strained southward through dancing, fierce

light for a sight of Sunflower. He had no serious misgivings about Fred Wheeler's scheme either, not even after he was within sight of the town and sensed the utterly quiet atmosphere down there. He had no reason to doubt Fred after all, twenty-seven years of facing down outlaws gave a man an edge.

He came down along the northward stage road feeling confident, feeling dehydrated but very close to the end of all his mid-summer riding, and hauled up as a man stepped out away from one of the yonder buildings at the end of town. A Winchester carbine slanted across the front of his body. That yonder man was scowling out at him as though seeking to identify Walt.

He reined back, unwilling to go closer until that armed man down there said something, called out or made a hostile move, or finished his dark staring. The armed man finally lowered his weapon, lifted his head, and called out.

"Hodge, come along!"

Walt eased his animal out. There had been something insistent in that shout, but nothing menacing. In fact, it almost sounded as though the armed man was relieved at identifying Walt.

He stopped again though, a hundred feet out, put his hand lightly upon the six-gun butt at his right side and wondered about that man down there. He was large and paunchy and thick. He was also vaguely familiar but not identifiably so.

"Who is it?" he called. "How did you know me, mister?"

"I'm the liveryman," said the armed man loudly. "I recognized that horse you're riding. He belongs to me. Come on. There's been hell bust loose here today."

Walt rode the last hundred feet with a sinking feeling behind his belt. He swung down near the armed liveryman, looked past as other figures became visible the length of Main Street, looked back, and waited.

"Fred Wheeler's been shot," said the liveryman. "He tried to arrest Mike Weedon's crew in town a couple hours back and the fireworks busted loose. I was with Fred . . . me and some of the other townsmen. It sure got hot around here for a while."

"Dead?" asked Walt, referring to Wheeler.

The liveryman shrugged. "He may be by now . . . I don't know. We packed him over to the jailhouse and made him as comfortable as we could. Luckily, the doctor was already over there."

"How did it happen?"

"Fred said you'd escaped and he wanted a posse to go after you. Six, seven of us fellows stepped forth. He deputized us . . . sort of . . . and we was getting saddled up when Mike Weedon and his bunch hit town. Fred come to my barn where we was to meet, said he was

120

going to arrest three of Mike's riders, and for us to come along and back his play." Here, the liveryman's eyes wavered before he continued his recital. "Some of the boys didn't want to buck Weedon."

Walt's lips drew downward. "Sure not," he growled. "Weedon was a pretty good source of free drinks over at the Variety House."

The liveryman let that go by. "Anyway," he continued, "Fred and three of us walked out into the roadway. I don't know exactly what happened next, Hodge. All I know is that someone fired a pistol. After that, Weedon's crew . . . they was still sittin' their saddles in front of the Variety House . . . cut loose. I think there was someone inside the saloon who'd run down the back alley from my place, run in down there, and called a warnin' to Mike. I don't know that's what happened though. All I'm sure of is that Fred wilted right at the first, when the firin' was heaviest. The rest of us ran back into my barn. Nothin' more happened for a long time so I snuck out, saw Weedon was gone with his boys, and got the others to help me pack poor old Fred down to his jailhouse. He stopped three slugs. One high up in the left arm, one in the left hip, and one alongside the head. We figured maybe that head shot cracked his skull."

The liveryman grounded his carbine, leaned upon it, and solemnly wagged his head back and forth. "Damnedest thing I ever seen take place in Sunflower and I've been here close to . . ."

"How did you know I might be coming along?"

"Huh? Oh, well, when we packed Fred down there, the sawbones give him smellin' salts or something. He come around. He said to watch for you. We thought he was still out of his head, but the sawbones said no. Fred told us what you and him had worked out. He told us why too. So we been waitin' around the edge of town and watchin'. Though we figured that you wouldn't show up until late tonight, even when Fred said to keep a watch anyway. I think he was afraid you'd stumble into Weedon."

"Here," said Walt, flinging the buckskin's reins at the liveryman without another word.

He hastened southward on into town. There were armed men here and there. None tried to stop him and only one started to speak as he hastened on past. Mostly, the townsmen seemed not to clearly understand what was going on. They acted like men who were prepared to resist force, but who did not exactly comprehend what that force was out to accomplish.

At the jailhouse Walt discovered several men lounging in the office, drinking coffee. They went silent the moment Walt entered, threw them a look, and headed on across to the cell-block. Someone had placed a hanging lamp in that dingy little corridor and here Walt encountered two more men. One of these was a worried-looking individual with a pin-striped shirt and sleeve garters who was also wearing the inappropriate combination of a derby hat and a storekeeper's apron. The second man was unmistakably a physician. He was standing there in conversation with the storekeeper, a coat draped over one arm, his physician's leather satchel clasped in both hands, looking gravely attentive at what his companion was saying.

These two looked up quickly as Walt came along. He saw them, too, but brushed on by and swung in where a cell door was open, saying nothing to either man.

Fred Wheeler was lying shirtless, hatless, and bootless. He had mounds of white bandaging material wrapped about him but his faded gaze was rational and steady despite the stain of discoloration along one side of his head and cheek.

He watched Walt lean down and said huskily: "Glad you showed up, boy. Looks like I guessed plumb wrong about Mike. The damned plan exploded in my face." He paused, then asked: "What you been up to?"

"Trying to set Bricker's crew afoot."

Wheeler's damp eyes, swimming in obvious pain, nevertheless flickered with faint approval. "Good," he mumbled. "That means all you got to do now is take my posse down to Weedon's place and arrest the lot of 'em for resisting arrest, attempted murder, suspicion of murder with malice, and anything else you can dream up."

Walt straightened back. "I can't do that," he said. "I haven't any authority. You said so yourself."

Wheeler raised a hand, opened it, and pushed his deputy's badge at Walt. "Take it," he said in a fading tone. "I already sent word to the sheriff I was goin' to appoint you my successor until he got someone else to come down here."

Walt took the badge, looked at it, looked back at the injured man, and puckered his forehead uneasily. "Is that legal?" he asked.

Wheeler mumbled a tart word. "Legal or not, we got to uphold the law, especially since Mike Weedon sure busted hell out of it in Sunflower today. You're dog-goned right it's legal, so you go get that whelp and his riders. I won't rest easy until I see him and his gun hawks in the cell next to mine."

Walt stood for a moment looking down and saying nothing.

The medical man came to the cell door and said: "I'm sorry, stranger, but Deputy Wheeler needs rest and quiet."

Walt drew in a big breath. Wheeler was watching him. When he saw that sigh, he muttered hoarsely: "Pin it on, Walt. You wanted to stop a range war. Well, boy, get out there and stop one."

Walt walked on out of the cell, past that storekeeper who'd heard all they said back and forth, on out into Wheeler's office where he stopped to consider the coffee-sipping townsmen. With a hard look at those men, he said: "Which one of you stood with Fred out in the roadway against Weedon?"

Four of those men looked at the ceiling, at one another, and said nothing.

But one man, a burly, sweaty man, rumbled: "I did. What of it?"

"You stay," ordered Walt. "The rest of you find some other place to loaf. Go on, get out of here."

As the townsmen gaped, Walt pinned on Wheeler's badge. Once they saw that, they got up and silently filed on out of the jailhouse. The burly man sat on, waiting. He had a truculent look to him and the physical power to back it up.

"What's your name?" asked Walt of this man who he had seen watching him from the blacksmith shop a number of times.

"Andy Blevins. What's yours?"

"Walt Hodge. Andy, I want a posse. Can you round one up?"

"Sure I can," said Blevins, rising up to stand thick-legged, his face clearing from its earlier truculence. "You takin' Fred's place?"

"Only for as long as it takes to bring in Mike Weedon and his trigger-happy riders."

Blevins's battered features broke into a pleased smile. "For that I can get the whole damned town," he assured Walt.

"No thanks," said Walt dryly. "Just fetch along men like yourself and the liveryman. We won't need any of those others who ran out when Wheeler needed them earlier."

Blevins nodded. "Now?" he said.

"Yeah, now. Armed and ready to ride."

Blevins's smile broadened. A fiery light danced up into his eyes. "I'll have 'em assembled at the livery barn in twenty minutes," he stated, and hurried on out of the office.

Walt considered that badge upon his shirt front. He'd never before worn such a symbol of authority and did not now relish the wearing of it.

But one thing was solidly in his mind now. He had tried several different ways to prevent a war here in Sunflower Valley, and while he'd been somewhat successful, he didn't believe anything more could be accomplished without force equal to the force Bricker and Weedon commanded. He went to the water bucket, lifted the dipper, and drank deeply.

All right, he told himself. *Those two firebrands need to be taught a rough lesson, and, as God is my witness I will now teach them one!*

He turned and walked out of the office, turned and hiked northward where men were beginning to excitedly gather under that bull-bass lash of Andy Blevins's waspish orders.

CHAPTER TWELVE

No one said much as Walt halted up there in front of the livery barn to consider the crew Andy Blevins had rounded up. Andy sauntered over, took a position at Walt's side, and awaited the judgment of Hodge.

That posse consisted of fifteen men. Only those fifteen had their horses at hand and bristled with armament, but easily another twenty men were also gathered there looking willing. After considering the faces around him, Walt concluded that Blevins knew his townsmen. There was not a man among those fifteen who did not look capable and willing to tangle with a buzz-saw.

"You did right," he told Blevins. "They look willing."

"They are," rasped the massive man at Walt's side. "I been blacksmith hereabouts for ten years. You don't shoe fellows' horses that long and not know which will and which won't. These here fellows will. You can take my word for that."

The liveryman walked over and handed Walt the reins to a fresh horse. Then he stood there waiting. Walt watched the others standing curiously around, recalled something Wheeler had said, made a rough gesture, and said to those bystanders: "Clear out. Go on back to your stores." After the others had retreated at least as far as the opposite plank walk, there to silently stand and watch, Walt said to his posse men: "You boys know where the Weedon Ranch is?"

Men nodded and muttered that they did.

"I don't," Walt stated, "so one of you'll have to lead the way. The thing to remember is . . . don't get split up and don't start a fight. If Weedon wants a fight, we'll give him all he wants, but let *him* start it."

A crusty older man said: "Fellows been known to get killed lettin' the other man have the first shot."

"I didn't say you had to let them have first shot, I said let them start it. We'll ride in and call on Weedon to come along peaceable. If he declines, then we smoke him out. But we don't start smokin' him out until he declines. That clear?"

"It's clear," said the same older man. "You're the boss, mister."

Blevins tapped Walt's arm and pointed with his blunt jaw northward. "We got company," Blevins muttered softly.

Others heard this as well as Walt turned to look northward up toward the far end of town.

Seven horsemen were walking their horses down the northward road toward Sunflower. They were no more than a quarter mile out when Walt and his posse men saw them.

"Bricker," someone said sharply. "Bricker and his B-Back-to-Back crew."

Walt stiffened. He had only seen Leila's father once before and that had been on foot and up close. He could not be sure of this identification, so he turned to Andy Blevins.

"Is it?" he asked.

"Yeah, it's Jim Bricker all right. He's even got his ranch cook along, too. Mister Hodge, I smell trouble here."

Walt knew instantly, after that positive identification had been made, that Leila had failed. Somehow she had been detected in her scheme to set her father and his riders afoot. He had to make a quick adjustment to this and he did.

"Boys," he said swiftly, "half of you cross to the east plank walk and take up positions over there in plain sight. Spread out so if there's shootin', you're not all bunched up. The other half of you stay on this side of the road and do the same . . . spread out thirty or forty feet apart."

The men, intently watching those oncoming riders, made no immediate move. Not until Blevins snarled in his bull-bass tone, then they began to move, to look doubtfully around to see which among them would go one way so they would know to go the other way. It was an almost leisurely break up of the posse men in front of the livery barn.

Blevins remained solidly at Walt's side. He

hooked both huge arms around his rifle and leaned there, squinting up where Bricker was just now riding between the northern-most sheds and shanties of Sunflower.

He said: "Mister Hodge, I know Jim Bricker. If you're figurin' on talkin' him out of anything, you ain't goin' to have any success. He's one of the most bull-headed men that ever lived."

Walt made no rejoinder to this. He was watching Bricker where the road narrowed. Bricker easily stayed out in front. His cowboys grouped up behind him. They were not saying a word now, nor did they increase the almost funereally slow pacing of their B-Back-to-Back horses. Walt grudgingly admired the solemn way Bricker was entering Sunflower. He knew perfectly well Bricker was deliberately doing this. Nothing would alert a town to danger as quickly as iron-faced horsemen entering slowly and riding through the same way. A dash, hooting yells, and flashing guns bewildered a town which was expecting nothing, but this, this slow-walking advance toward Sunflower's center, it gave every timid person plenty of time to get away. It also gave every doubting person enough time to make up his mind that whatever was coming, he did not necessarily have to become involved.

"He's smart," said Walt to Andy Blevins. "He's doing this on purpose."

"Smart's only half of it," grumbled Blevins, his eyes pinched nearly closed and sweat making his scarred face shiny with grease. "He's also a bad man to cross. He'll fight, Mister Hodge. In fact, if I had to take my pick between Mike Weedon and Jim Bricker, I'd say Bricker would be the toughest to battle with in more ways than one."

"Andy, you sure those men you rounded up won't panic?"

"No fear there, Mister Hodge. I hand-picked these fellows. I saw what happened before with Fred Wheeler, so I picked these fellows just for somethin' like this, and there ain't a man among 'em I haven't known at least ten years. They won't run, even if Bricker starts throwin' lead. No, sir. I can just about promise you that."

Bricker had now come far enough south into town to see the armed men lining both sides of the roadway at long intervals. He seemed almost to check his horse at this sight, but he didn't, he kept right on riding. He'd also seen powerful Andy Blevins, the blacksmith, and Walt Hodge, the man he believed was responsible for his range boss's death, standing together out in the roadway in front of the livery barn with the bitter, yellow sunlight limning them. Still, Bricker neither said anything to the men behind him nor altered his slow-pacing advance.

Sunflower, behind the lined-up posse men, fearfully and hurriedly began putting up shutters over its glass windows. Shoppers who moments before had been lethargically passing back and forth, seemed suddenly to have quite dissolved. There were no pedestrians in sight anywhere the full length of Main Street. Even horse, wagon, and buggy traffic was suddenly no longer in sight.

Blevins looked around and back again without moving more than his upper half, then he made a cold chuckle that rumbled like distant thunder deep down. "Ol' Jim's sure done it," he told Walt. "The danged town's went to cover like a broom-tailed fox. You could shoot a cannon straight down Main Street and not hit a soul . . . man or critter."

Walt was looking up where those oncoming horsemen were progressing close enough to make out features, expressions, armament. They were still several squares off but it was midday now with no shadows except directly underfoot and things stood out sharply to a man's anxious stare.

He was jarred to recognize one of those riders up there as being the same Foster Babcock he and Leila had left bound to a tree up at the little spring. There were ugly implications to this. Unless Babcock had gotten free by himself, then somehow Leila had told where he was, which also meant she'd had to explain at least part of why he'd been tied there.

Since her father obviously knew some of that affair, he probably had surmised more of it, because Babcock would have told him. This, Walt thought now, would account for some of the storminess he could distantly make out on those two faces—Babcock's youthful face and Jim Bricker's fiery, rock-hard, older face.

Blevins too saw, and perhaps sensed, something here, for he said softly: "Goin' to be hell to pay, Mister Hodge. Jim's mad to the marrow and his riders don't look much different."

"He wants me," Walt murmured. "He still thinks I killed his range boss."

"Well," said Blevins matter-of-factly, "didn't you?"

Walt turned in surprise. "Do you believe that?" he asked. "Do the others?"

Blevins met Walt's stare and shrugged. "No one's told us different yet. All we know is that Fred said you were to be trusted. Personally, I figured you must've killed him in a fair fight . . . some way."

"He was shot in the back."

Blevins assumed a doggedly stubborn look. "All I know is that Fred said you was to be trusted. That's good enough for me. I guess it's good enough for the others, too, otherwise they wouldn't be backin' you up with their guns right now."

Walt twisted to gaze right and left. Not a one

of those sentinel posse men had moved out of his place. Every head was turned toward Bricker's men and every face was toughly resolute.

"I'll be damned," murmured Walt.

Blevins's face creased into a strained small smile. "You damned well may be before this is over, friend," he muttered.

"Let me ask you a question, Andy. When Fred told the lot of you at the livery barn he was going to arrest three of Mike Weedon's riders, didn't he tell you why?"

"Nope. And afterward things happened too fast for us to ask a lot of questions. Mister Hodge, Fred Wheeler's been the law here in Sunflower since long before most of us can remember. He's honest and straightforward. If he says someone's got to be arrested, that's plenty good for them of us as he picks to back his play."

Walt continued to regard the blacksmith's dark and scarred profile for a moment longer, then, feeling no more doubt about these men who he'd called upon to support him, he faced fully around northward again.

Blevins, without taking his gaze off those oncoming riders, said quietly: "You feelin' a little better now, Mister Hodge?"

"One hundred percent better, Andy."

"That's good, 'cause a fellow can't fight good unless he's got confidence in them around him. I know. I was in the war."

These two said no more for a while. Not until Jim Bricker was only one square away and had his full attention riveted upon them where they still stood in the fierce sunlight in front of the livery barn.

Then Walt said almost gently: "I think you're right, Andy. I don't believe we're going to be able to talk him out of this."

"Sure not. I knew that the minute I seen him out there comin' into town with his full crew."

Somewhere behind Main Street a dog began to frantically bark. This sound broke into the hush with a jarring edginess. A man's sharp voice swearing at the dog also sounded unusually loud.

Walt noticed that he could suddenly see things with unusual clarity. Each detail of those approaching horsemen stood out starkly in his sight. His hearing was better too and even his sense of smell. In fact, every aroma rising from that heat-seared roadway was sharp-cut and distinguishable from every other scent.

His body seemed cold despite the piled up heat beating upon him—cold and completely relaxed and efficient. He had no fear in him at all, but neither did he feel any anger. He was coldly calm and rational. He thought that he would have to watch for anything Bricker might do; that he must somehow find an opening which would enable him to prevent a gunfight here in the center of Sunflower and, for some reason he did not attempt to analyze, he felt completely confident that he was going to be able to do this.

Bricker was less than a hundred feet away now. He came on another sixty feet, raised his rein hand, and stopped. All those other men followed suit. The hush was almost unbearable.

CHAPTER THIRTEEN

Jim Bricker was normally red-faced and solid, but today, under that fierce overhead faded old sun he seemed more solid and redder. Only his eyes were clear and they became unblinkingly fixed upon Walter Hodge with an intensity that was nearly physical. Walt braced into that uncompromising glare, waiting. At his side Andy Blevins was like stone. He was no longer leaning upon his rifle; he now held the gun in both hands low across his body. He could have been standing there casually or standing there dangerously; it was one of those stances which could be interpreted in whatever way an onlooker wished.

"Hodge," said Bricker in a voice like steel, "you're going to wish you'd never come here after today. I don't know how you got out of jail or how you got Fred Wheeler's badge, but those things aren't going to matter. You're a murderer and worse. Toss down your gun and take off the badge."

Walt looked past Bricker into those other faces around him. Every B-Back-to-Back man was sitting his saddle like a puppet, a wire-tight puppet wound to explode into violent action at the first sign. He looked back at Leila's father feeling as a man feels who walks upon thin ice.

"Wheeler's been shot," he said quietly, distinctly. "He authorized me to take his place. As for my being out of jail, Bricker, if you'd listened to your daughter, you'd know by now that I didn't kill your range boss."

"I listened to her," said Bricker, his voice flattening out, sounding bitter and bleak. "You turned her head, Hodge. You deliberately went out of your way to use my girl, to turn her against her own father. I'll kill you for that if it's the last thing I ever do."

Walt sucked back a breath. "I didn't use her, Bricker. Every word I told her was the truth. You won't believe that . . . I won't expect you to. But she's out of this now." Walt paused, then took the plunge. "Bricker, you've made a fool of yourself by refusing to recognize the truth."

"The truth!" snarled Jim Bricker.

"Yes, the truth. Though, as I said, I don't expect you to believe it. You're a stubborn fool. You're going to get some men killed the minute you make a move, and for nothing. Go ask Fred Wheeler what's true and what isn't."

"You said he was dead."

"I said he'd been shot, Bricker. You don't hear very good, or else you've just jumped to another false conclusion. Go ask him. He's with the doctor down at the jailhouse. But whether you go or not, let me tell you one thing. You and these men of yours are going to dismount right here, put down your guns, and be locked up until Mike Weedon's rounded up. There'll be no range war in Sunflower Valley."

For the first time a flicker of something close to doubt showed in Jim Bricker's eyes. He looked once at Andy Blevins standing there, watching him, on over at the nearest hard-faced townsmen with their guns at the ready, then back to Walt.

He said: "You want a fight, don't you, Hodge. You want to make a big show in front of these folks down here at Sunflower. You've got them eating out of your hand, too, like you have my daughter. Well . . ."

"Yes?"

"You're going to get it, Hodge."

Someone on the east side of the roadway cocked a gun.

That harsh small sound carried easily in the stillness to every man out in the pitilessly sun-seared roadway. Bricker heard it, too, and licked his lips. A man would have to be an idiot to be up there where Bricker was sitting between two ranks of armed men and not know he was the target of every eye around him. His riders too could not but have sensed the danger around them.

Walt shook his head. "You're stubborn and brave," he said. "But I don't believe you're a fool, Bricker. Move one hand, let one of your men move a hand, and the lot of you'll die right here in this roadway. That's a fact and you can see that it is."

"You won't be around afterward though," said Bricker.

Now for the first time Andy Blevins spoke. His rumbling, deep, rough voice carried the full resonance of distant cannon fire.

"Mister Bricker, nothing's goin' to change if you and Mister Hodge get killed, except that maybe us fellows from Sunflower will be shy some pretty good men. Fact is, Mister Bricker, ten or fifteen dead men won't resolve a blessed thing here."

"Keep out of this," growled Jim Bricker, without even glancing at Blevins. "Hodge, tell your men to put aside their guns."

"I'm afraid I can't do that. This is their town. They have every right to defend it."

"I don't care about their town. It's you I want. You and Mike Weedon."

Walt was silent for a moment, then he said: "Bricker, I've kept you and Weedon apart up to now to save some lives, I guess I can do it again. You sure it's not just me you want?"

"Dead sure."

Walt did an unexpected thing. He unbuckled his shell belt and dropped it in the roadway which raised a cloud of dust. He then called Jim Bricker a fighting name right before he said: "Get down off that horse and rake me then," he said. "Unless you're yellow without those guns to back you up."

No one had expected things to turn this personal, this private and individual, so no one said anything, but all those wire-tight faces swung and every eye ran from Walt to the thickly made Jim Bricker who sat his saddle woodenly, considering his challenger.

"If you win," Walt said, "I'll do what you say. If I win, you and your men will do as I say."

Bricker solidly shook his head at this. "You got nothing to bargain with. You're nothing but a lousy back-shooter and a . . ."

"You yellow, Mister Bricker?" asked Andy Blevins, interrupting to softly ask this. "Hodge's made what seems to me to be a right fair offer." Blevins looked at those intently watching B-Back-to-Back men. "You boys think your boss ought to let a man call him what Hodge just called him, and not fight?"

None of Bricker's men answered. They didn't appear to even have heard what Andy said, but this deluded no one. Arizonans knew the ways of violence. Whether those men spoke up or not, in their minds Jim Bricker had to fight.

Blevins looked back up at Bricker. "No man ever had to challenge me twice," he said. "And unless I sure figured you wrong all these years, Mister Bricker, no one's goin' to have to call you out twice either."

Walt stood there waiting. He felt that he'd scored in perhaps the only way he could have. He'd allowed Bricker to say openly that this was a personal feud, then he'd accepted that and flung down his personal challenge. Bricker obviously understood this too, understood how he'd been out-maneuvered, had been cut loose from his supporting guns. He was rigid up there atop his horse and scarcely breathing. Hate for one man seemed near to choking him.

He swung out and landed down hard in the dusty roadway. He unbuckled his gun belt, let it fall, removed his hat, and clapped it over his saddle horn. Sunlight flamed where it touched his red mane. His big mottled hands opened and closed, and Walt, watching all this, knew he was in for the battle of his life. Bricker would kill him if he possibly could. He wouldn't stop at just beating Walt senseless, he would blind him with taloned fingers, choke him to death with powerful arms, he would break Walt's neck or his back, and he'd gloat while doing it . . . if he could.

The sweat-oily atmosphere roundabout those two changed. Blevins and his armed townsmen changed their stances a little and put their attention upon Walt and Jim Bricker. Those B-Back-to-Back men atop their saddles also left off speculating about the armed townsmen and concentrated upon their employer and the slightly lighter, younger man facing Bricker. From behind doors and windows, observers peered out from places up and down Main Street, straining to see whatever ensued.

No one paid the slightest attention to a rider far out southward who appeared almost as a wraith as he came along in a punishing jog through layers of faded yellow brightness. No one even saw him among those men there in the center of Main Street, nor would they have heeded his advance even if they had, for, here and now, Sunflower's vortex of imminent violence had settled upon just those two opposing men, one older, one younger, one scarred and seasoned and oaken, the other youthful and standing calmly.

Blevins spoke softly in his rumbling bass as those two took measure of each other. To the B-Back-to-Back men and those townsmen lining opposite plank walks, he said: "No interference, boys. It'll be a fair fight."

Walt watched Bricker's rugged face. He saw a shadow pass across it as though something had just occurred to the older man. Bricker's deep-set eyes, though, remained icy. He seemed to be considering Walt for signs of strength and weakness.

Bricker started forward away from his horse. In a moment he was out of that animal's weak shade where full sunlight struck him, but in the same moment there was a sudden diversion.

"Stop it," a quick, sharp voice said from off to one side. "Father, stop it!"

Involuntarily all those heads swung, all those eyes looked astonished for each man had recognized that female voice with its high shrillness and its tearing anguish. It sounded completely out of place here, completely foreign to this moment of savage sun and dust and violence.

Bricker, in the act of taking another onward step, settled his foot in the roadway dust and turned. Walt also looked over where Leila was striding ahead from between two buildings, her face flushed, her eyes dry and hot and full of naked, raw agony.

"Stay out of this," Bricker ordered.

Leila walked on, her nostrils flaring with temper, her blouse lifting and falling, until she was no more than ten feet off. When she halted finally, she turned her full bitterness upon her father, saying in a rush of unsteady words: "You can't ever be wrong can you? I told you not to do this . . . I asked you to make sure first. But no . . . you rode into Sunflower just this far . . . just until you saw *him*. You wouldn't listen, would you? You wouldn't really try to find out because you felt Walt had topped you and that's one thing you can't stand, isn't it, for anyone who opposes you to be right!"

All those silent men looked and seemed

embarrassed. Something which detracted from the purely masculine moment was suddenly thrust upon them. They didn't know what to do about it, exactly, and they sat or stood and looked glum and uneasy.

Without looking away from his daughter, Bricker said savagely to one of his mounted riders, calling this man by name. "Ben, take her away from here. Keep her out of this."

That cowboy eased off as though to dismount. He had his right boot swinging free of the stirrup when Andy Blevins growled another order at that man.

"Stay where you are, fellow. Don't get off that horse."

Caught in mid-motion, the cowboy turned still. Blevins looked over at Leila, his tone softening to a deep growl. "It's got to be this way," he told her. "Let them have it out, Miss Leila. The alternative is to see maybe six, eight dead men in the roadway. Walt's still tryin' to keep it from comin' down to that, girl. Don't change it now. Go back or stay where you are, but don't say another word."

Blevins kept watching Leila. So did Walt and Leila's father. She had become a focal point for all that attention, but there appeared no awareness of this on her face, in her eyes. She appeared instead to be balancing Blevins's words.

Walt saw her wilt a little, run an anguished

look out at him. He nodded slightly, telling her unmistakably in this silent manner that Andy Blevins was right.

Leila looked with bitterness out where her father still stood.

She said to him almost harshly: "I hope you lose. I hope he beats you senseless for what you're trying to do to all these people." She swung about and passed beyond sight back the way she'd come.

For a moment longer Jim Bricker stood there, half twisted from the waist, looking after his only child. Walt thought there was something sagging in the older man's look, in his stance, but was not sure because Bricker straightened back around, his face the same in its ferocity, in its terrible resolve and determination. Bricker started forward again. He stopped when no more than twenty feet separated him from Walt, brought up big, scarred, and freckled fists, and looked over them dead ahead.

Walt moved now for the first time. He stepped once to the left, once to the right, presenting the side of his body as he did this, making both a smaller target for those oaken fists and also forcing Bricker to change stance each time he moved, forcing Bricker to concentrate upon his footing and not his immediate striking power.

Bricker's face smoothed out. He showed in his expression that he'd just made a discovery.

This younger man was not going to be the easy conquest Bricker had thought. Obviously, Walt Hodge was also experienced in this business of brawling.

Bricker waited. When Walt stopped moving, Bricker moved up another few feet. His right shoulder dropped the slightest bit until its full force lay directly behind that lethal cocked right fist.

Walt moved again, this time to the left, forcing Bricker to raise that dropped shoulder. Bricker's face flamed red.

"Fight, damn you!" he exclaimed. "Stand and fight!"

Walt stopped moving, faced fully around, and set himself. It was as though he had just agreed to meet Bricker on Bricker's own terms.

Chapter Fourteen

There was a crimson splotch across Jim Bricker's face now, as much, Walt thought, from the dehydrating heat of the roadway as from the man's terrible wrath. Bricker began his solid advance. When he was less than three feet away, he cocked that right fist again, dropped his left arm across his upper body protectively, and swung.

Walt turned only his head. The fist grazed him, turning him instantly cold with this initial shock of combat as he was stung. Warning flashed instantly to his every nerve end. Bricker was a powerful man. He knew how to move in his full weight behind his fists.

Walt lashed out lightly, twice drove Bricker back and half turned as though to move, then didn't move, but instead brought up a solid blow that caught Bricker off guard a little and rocked him.

Their first exchange was over. Each man stepped clear, began shuffling. All those bystanders, trying to judge who'd gotten the best of this first encounter, stood totally silent and motionless except one old man who had crept from between two buildings to stop behind the armed townsmen. This old man's fisted hands jerked, his body swayed and danced in and out. He was living this fight blow by blow and move by countermove. No one heeded him at all.

Bricker suddenly drove his body straight at Hodge. He swung when he was close enough and grunted with this effort. He bored in flailing away, grunting. Walt stepped sideways, then back again, caught Bricker flush on the cheek, and stepped away again, letting the older man whip past and come around.

Now Bricker dropped both arms, stood with his head slightly to one side studying Walt, then started forward once more. This time Walt gave no ground. This time he meant to test endurance with Bricker, and everyone watching those two guessed it was to be this way by Walt's solid, knee-sprung stance. He was flat-footed, his shoulders rolled up in support of raised fists, and his head was dropped low and tucked into the curve of his upper arm and shoulder.

Bricker came on, at the last moment side-stepped, and as Walt twisted, Bricker jumped back and came in. He went in beating past Walt's guard and sledging a powerful blow straight ahead. Walt caught that staggering punch over the heart and gave ground in a series of unsteady maneuvers. He'd been hurt. Bricker kept on. One of his strikes grazed upward along Walt's cheek and lost its force in his hair. Another blow ripped in low, grated across Walt's forearm, and sank deep into the younger man's unprotected middle.

Walt gave more ground until he had his back within ten feet of the livery barn's front wall. He turned his side toward Bricker absorbing that punishment along the ribs, the hip, the left shoulder. He kept his head moving. He cracked Bricker along the jaw. Bricker sagged just for an instant, but his recovery was fast. He had the initiative and fought on to keep it. He took another light punch in the face, dropped his face like a bull, and waggled his head. Walt's third blow was lower. It caught Bricker in the soft parts even as Leila's father was bringing up his guard to protect his face and upper body. That time Bricker was stopped. Breath whooshed out of him. He stubbornly refused to give ground though and fought back to retain his initiative.

Walt tried sidling away so he could not be pinned to the barn wall, but Bricker was on him in an instant, striking, pushing, grunting, purple-faced and wild. He got in so close his shoulder point struck Walt, knocking him back. His head struck rough board siding and a roaring ensued inside his skull.

Bricker's purple features with their wild eyes came close enough for Walt to feel the man's hot breath. He rolled his head and kept it moving. He tried once more to sidle away from being pinned, but Bricker dropped down and came in low using his solid and considerable weight as a battering ram. He struck Walt hard, carried him against the building, forced his lowered head into Walt's chest, and pumped both his arms in and out, in and out, without aim or direction but with unmistakable purpose.

Walt, smothered for this moment, tried once again to present his side to those sledging strikes. Bricker held him pinned though with his greater weight. Walt took the shock of those punishing fists a moment longer, then got one hand up under Bricker's jaw, strained to force the man's head back, and when he succeeded, Bricker's wild blows began to miss. Bricker tried jumping clear. Walt chopped him in the face. He brought up a strike from the lower regions that popped solidly upon Bricker's chin. He wrestled Bricker backward from the barn wall, jumped back a foot, and levelled a savage right hand. Bricker saw this punch coming. He dropped down to get under it and half succeeded, but, still, the force of that blow sent him off balance, knocking him farther away.

Walt was after the older man now, his breath hissing in and out, audible to all those rooted spectators. He battered Bricker twice in the face, twice over the heart, four times hard in the middle. He kept this barrage coming until Bricker's guard, useless because the older man never knew where the next blow would strike, began to weaken, to move up and down, left and right so that all Walt had to do was wait for each move, then strike Bricker where he was not guarded.

One of those B-Back-to-Back men made a loud groan. Over on the west sidewalk that old man was jerking drunkenly, gasping and writhing as though he and not Jim Bricker was taking that bruising punishment. Andy Blevins's normally ruddy, bronzed features were strained white and like stone. His little sunk-set eyes were alight with a primitive eagerness. There was something ancient and primordial in his locked-down expression.

Walt came around on Bricker's left and struck him. He jumped to the man's right and struck him again. Bricker had lost his initiative. He was now defending himself. He must have realized, as all those other rough men also knew, that no man ever won a fight by being entirely defensive, and yet each time he attempted to push out of that cloudy world which seemed now to be claiming him a little at a time, a rock fist exploded against him somewhere with the hurting force of a swung axe handle.

Walt suddenly danced away, his breathing making a raw, rasping sound in the awful silence and scuffed-up dust of the roadway.

"Call it off," he gasped at Jim Bricker.

Bricker's one good eye glowed with stubborn but subdued fire. He called Walt a fierce name.

"Come at it," he said. "I'll kill you, Hodge. Damn you . . . I'll kill you with my hands."

Andy Blevins bristled. "Go get him, boy," he said to Walt. "You give him his chance. Now go get the whelp!"

A B-Back-to-Back rider said something in a low tone and Blevins turned, his columnar neck corded and eager. He fixed that rider with his tawny stare and flintily said: "All right, mister, you're next. As soon as this is over, you're next."

Bricker made a heavy rush on Walt which brought him close, then on by the place where Walt no longer was. Bricker swung back and tried again. Walt waited until the last possible moment, sucked back, lunged in as Bricker rocked past, and landed a blow behind the older man's ear. Bricker stumbled, kept on stumbling along until his momentum ended, then he came around and hung over there with most of the focus gone from that one unclosed eye. Claret dripped from his smashed lips, from a puffy cut beside his closed eye. He was sucking back enormous amounts of insufficient, hot mid-summer dry air. He was a ruin to gaze upon.

Walt had two purpling swellings upon his face, one passing upward into his hair from the right cheek, one along the side of his left jaw. His right fist was relatively unbruised but his left hand was bluish from broken-open knuckles. His eyes were cloudy with pain, with numbing physical exhaustion, but he started for Jim Bricker again with steady, springy steps. He couldn't keep this up much longer, but he would find some inner source for the little bit more energy he required.

Bricker threw a slow punch and blocked a slow strike with a forearm. He was fighting defensively again, and he was also fighting mechanically. He was going through the motions without seeming to care whether he connected or not. Walt shouldered past that forearm guard, cracked Bricker over the bridge of the nose, cracked him full in the mouth, squared around as Bricker sagged, cracked him low in the stomach, and saw the older man's shoulders and arms drop, saw his one opened eye roll up and around aimlessly. Almost expended, Walt attempted to hold back Bricker's pawing and put all his remaining force into a chilling, paralyzing strike that, when it came in, made a meaty echo as Walt's arm sank wrist-deep into the other man's soft parts.

Bricker's knees sprung outward, a sob wrenched deep up out of him. He threw out both hands as though to brace himself, as though to catch himself. Walt pushed them aside, caught Bricker's sodden shirt front, heaved the older man completely around, and gave him a hard push. Bricker went over backward, struck the roadway, causing a burst of soiled dust, and sobbed again. Under the glazed stare of all those

155

onlookers he scrabbled in the dirt with both hands, got half up, then collapsed face down and did not move again.

For a time no one moved. Walt stood wide-legged out there fighting for oxygen, his shirt a rag flapping at his waist, that furious sun mercilessly showing every red welt, every fist imprint.

Andy Blevins turned and growled at someone behind him to fetch a bucket of water from within the barn. This was done, but Andy did not himself walk out and sponge Walt off; he ordered another man to do this while he turned, still with his rifle in both hands, and watched those motionless B-Back-to-Back riders. He singled out that one particular man with whom he'd earlier had words.

"Get down off that gawd-damned horse," he said to this man. "You touch that gun . . . any of you . . . and there'll be six dead cowboys to bury before sunset. You up there, I said get down."

But this man did not dismount. He seemed to shrink into himself. If there had ever been any fight in him there was none now. He avoided looking down at Blevins with absolute and undeviating resolution. Blevins recognized that this man was whipped before he'd started. He said no more, but his mouth drew contemptuously downward for as long as he continued to watch those mounted men.

Walt felt the sting of water where his skin was torn. He didn't look at the man sponging him off with a smelly rag, but instead concentrated upon the relief that came gradually to erode away his former feeling of near suffocation.

Another man came lugging a water bucket, but this one had a glum, bitter expression on his face. He came from the direction of the Dallas House, wore a barman's apron, and clearly was one of those watchers who'd observed that titanic battle from behind some safe shelter. Just as clearly too, this man had lost money on Jim Bricker, for when he halted beside the unconscious, fallen cowman, he grimaced with savage pleasure as he up-ended his bucket over Bricker, then turned and went stamping back toward the Dallas House.

Andy Blevins looked round at his sentinels upon the opposite sidewalks. He lifted his head and said: "All right. Every one of you heard the terms . . . if Bricker lost, him and his men do as Mister Hodge tells 'em. Now show your weapons, boys, 'cause I'm goin' to commence draggin' rough and tough B-Back-to-Backers off from their horses if they don't do what they're told."

Blevins faced those mounted men. On both sides of the roadway townsmen raised pistols, carbines, even a shotgun or two. Several of those men also cocked their guns.

Jim Bricker's cowboys dismounted without

a word or without any hesitation. They had the thoroughly demoralizing and stark picture twenty feet ahead of them of their powerful, arrogant employer lying in muddy dust as beaten as any man any of them had ever seen. They had no fight left in them at all.

"Drop those gun belts!"

Blevins waited until this order had also been obeyed before pacing over where someone had brought Walt a fresh shirt and was standing there as Walt put it on.

Blevins said: "How d'you feel, Mister Hodge?" His tone was solicitous, entirely different from the tone he'd used to the B-Back-to-Backers not ten seconds before.

"Dry," responded Walt with a lop-sided grin. "Dry enough to drink a lake plumb dry, Andy."

Andy turned and bawled for water and a dipper. He turned back and said: "You won fair and square. You want these men locked up at the jailhouse, Mister Hodge?"

Walt turned, his face discolored and swelling, his mouth a little smashed, the concluded fight still a smoky haze in his gaze.

"Yeah, Andy. Him too." Walt nodded toward Jim Bricker. He held that smoky glance upon the beaten man in the nearby dust for a moment, then seemed to recall something, seemed to wish suddenly his rummaging glance might light upon someone else.

Andy Blevins, seeing this, said quietly: "In the livery barn office, Mister Hodge. I seen her go in there." Andy put forth a hand, laid it gently upon Walt, and gently squeezed. "Go explain how it had to be, boy. You're the only one as can. The rest of it, don't worry . . . us boys will take care of the rest of it."

CHAPTER FIFTEEN

Leila was where Andy Blevins had said she was.

When Walt's shadow darkened the dingy door-way of the barn's horse sweat–scented, gloomy, small office she raised her head. She didn't seem surprised to see Walt standing there instead of her father, and looked steadily up without speaking.

"It had to be that way," he gently said, moving into the room with leaden steps. "Leila, I don't care what the others think, but, with you, it's different. I want you to understand that if I hadn't figured some way to make your father turn this into a personal fight between the two of us, a lot of men might have died out there. And for no real reason."

"I understand," she murmured, looking shaken and dull-eyed. "I rode up when you two were talking in the roadway. I knew, Walt. I understood what you were doing. Only, I was terribly afraid."

Leila stood up, half turned away, and placed both hands upon the desk top in front of her.

"I know my father better than anyone. He has his faults, but I love him, Walt. Those things I said to him . . . I meant them . . . but they don't change how I feel about him. Do you understand what I'm saying?"

"Sure, Leila."

She swung fully around and scanned his damaged face, saw the shadows of near total exhaustion in his eyes. She went over to him and put a cool hand to his right cheek where the worst of the swelling was.

"What do we do now?" she asked gravely.

"*We* don't do anything, Leila. You stay here in town or go back to the ranch, but I'm going after Weedon. One part of this range feud is over. The other part's yet to be taken care of."

"No, Walt, don't do that. You're going to run out of luck."

He reached for her. She went willingly up against him, put her cheek to his chest, and relaxed.

"There's no one else, Leila. Weedon's men shot Fred Wheeler."

"Let the townsmen do it. Let Andy Blevins do it."

"It's not their fight."

She pushed back looking up into his face. "It's not your fight, either. Mike Weedon started it. Let him finish it."

"You don't know what you're saying. Weedon's the only one left loose, Leila. He'll have it all his own way. We can't have that. He killed your range boss . . . at least his men did. They also shot down Fred Wheeler. If they're left free now, the next place they strike might be right here in Sunflower."

"It's not your town or mine either, Walt."

He held her at arms' length and gently shook her. "But it's not the town's fault, Leila. Right now I've got the authority to stop Weedon. I've also got the men. What kind of a man would I be if I didn't even try?"

"A live one, Walt. I love a live man. Don't make me a widow even before . . ."

"I'll come back. You wait here in town. I'll come back for you." Walt dropped his arms, he faintly scowled down at her. "I can't believe in a destiny that would lead a man this close to something he's been waiting all his life for, then let him get killed."

Her gaze turned misty with unshed tears. She said nothing for a moment. She turned, crossed to a battered old chair, and sank down. She whispered: "I'm drained dry. I feel old and robbed of everything I've cherished, Walt. If anything happens to you . . . it will all be true."

He crossed to her chair, leaned down, tilted up her face, and brushed her lips with his battered mouth. Then he straightened around and, without saying anything, passed on out of the livery barn office, out of the barn itself into the shimmering roadway, and scarcely saw the people who thirty minutes before had not been anywhere around. He walked down as far as Fred Wheeler's jailhouse and pushed wearily inside.

At once the current of voices in that airless

place rushed over him. Townsmen in the deputy's outer office looked up and said nothing.

Andy Blevins, emerging from over at the cell-block entrance, paused in his stride and ceased swinging a brass ring of big keys.

"Glad you're here," said Andy. "Fred wants to see you."

Walt crossed over. "You locked up the others?" he asked.

Blevins nodded, his smoldering gaze not yet calmed away from what he'd been through out in the roadway. "I locked 'em up and the doc looked at Bricker." Andy pursed his lips. "You sure beat him. He's got a busted nose, two teeth knocked out, and a torn ear."

"Is he conscious?"

"Yeah. Doc fetched him around. But a fellow can't understand him when he tries to talk. In the next cell, Fred called him every name he could lay his tongue to, which is quite a roster of names. He told Bricker what a fool he'd been, and how you wasn't no murderer, that it was Weedon's men shot Bricker's range boss. Fred's madder than a wet hen."

"Yeah," muttered Walt, and started past.

But Blevins halted him with more words. "You want to keep the posse rounded up and ready to ride?"

Walt nodded, made a grimace, and half humorously, half seriously, said: "If Weedon's

163

place is more than five miles from here, I'll never make it."

Blevins started to speak, turned as a small commotion erupted over at the roadside door, and darkly scowled at a dusty, sweaty newcomer who pushed his way inside.

"What the hell d'you want?" the blacksmith growled at this newcomer.

"To see Fred Wheeler," answered up the sweaty cowboy. "I been ridin' in from the south for two hours under that damned deadly sun, Blevins, and I got something to tell Fred. It won't keep, neither."

There was a quick urgency in this cowboy's voice that escaped none of the men in that room.

Walt Hodge stepped away from Blevins, back toward the center of the office, saying: "You can tell me, cowboy. I'm substituting for Wheeler until he can be up and around again. What is it?"

"You're Hodge, ain't you?" said the newcomer. "I heard about you at the Dallas House when I got a drink of cold beer up there a few minutes ago."

Walt looked impatient. He didn't reply to that obviously unnecessary question. "What is it? What news have you for Deputy Wheeler?" he demanded.

"Mike Weedon's comin'."

That room full of men became instantly hushed. Every man stared at the newly arrived cowboy.

164

Andy Blevins strode up beside Walt, his face darkening. "Coming here," he demanded. "Comin' here to Sunflower?"

"Yes."

"You saw him?" asked Walt.

"Plain as day. I was ridin' the range south a few miles. I seen Weedon's bunch east of me a ways. I thought it might be them, so I rode closer to make plumb sure. You see, I heard about Fred Wheeler gettin' winged. Some fellows passin' my camp this morning told me. They said Weedon's crew done it. So when I seen 'em headin' this way, I naturally got curious. After I made plumb sure, I come a-dustin' it for town to warn Fred they're probably comin' back to finish what they started with him."

The cowboy stopped speaking, squinted triumphantly at those still, expressionless faces, then he said: "I was ridin' in from the south when that danged fight was goin' on. Hell, if I'd just hurried a little, I'd have got to see that too."

Walt looked at Andy Blevins. The blacksmith was watching their informant over by the door.

Blevins growled at that rider: "Go buy yourself another drink and get out of here."

The cowboy looked surprised and indignant. He started to say something in quick protest, but Blevins's head-on stare decided him against this. The cowboy turned and went stumping out of the jailhouse.

"I know him," said Andy to Walt's inquiring look. "He's tellin' the truth. He'd ride fifty miles to watch a shootin' or a brawl, and it would tickle him silly if someone got killed or beat half to death, but he's no liar. Weedon's ridin' for Sunflower all right."

The doctor appeared across the room in the cell-block doorway. He looked straight at Walt.

"Fred wants to see you," he said. "He heard that about Mike Weedon returning."

Walt left the others, standing or sitting in total silence out in the office, passed along toward Wheeler's cot, and saw the pale, demoralized faces of Bricker's riders looking owlishly out as he strode past. Bricker himself did not look up. He was flat out upon the cot in that adjoining cell with bandages applied to his wounds.

Wheeler seemed much better. His head was still badly swollen, the bandages were colored scarlet in places, but his muddy eyes showed hard fire as Walt eased down upon the edge of his cot.

"Now you got your work cut out for you," the lawman said. "You may have beat Bricker, but Weedon's expectin' trouble. He'll be different. He won't be ridin' in straight up like Bricker did. Listen . . . he won't do much to the town and you've already proved yourself to everyone here. Why don't you head out for the county seat and tell the sheriff what's happened down here. Tell

166

him this here is a gun town now and we got to have some . . ."

"How far to the county seat?" asked Walt softly, cutting across that rush of angry words. "How far, Fred?"

"Well . . ."

"How far?"

"Thirty miles."

"You know dog-goned well I'd never get there and back in time to do any of you any good." Walt smiled. "Thanks for the suggestion, anyway. But I figure I'll stick, Fred. I sort of brought this thing on, so I'll stick around and see it through to its ending."

"You're pushin' your luck, boy," intoned the grizzled lawman.

"Maybe. You and I got an agreement, remember? You do the thinking, I do the leg work."

Wheeler snorted. He kept watching Walt's face, skeptically gauging the bruises there and the purple swellings.

"I believe you could take Mike," he mused. "In an even fight, mind you. But, Walt, you're battered from stem to stern from tanglin' with Bricker. You got no business goin' up against Weedon, too. Especially in the shape you're in."

Walt arose. "You sound like someone else I just talked to, Fred, and I got the same answer for both of you. This is how things have got to be. This is how they've worked out. I'm square in the middle and I can only go one way . . . and that's on through to the last bugle, Fred. That other person didn't understand how this has to be, but you understand."

Wheeler let his head ease back. "Leila . . . ?" he asked softly.

"Yeah, Leila."

"She's here in town?"

"Yes."

"Go get her," said Deputy Wheeler. "There's only one building in all Sunflower built to deflect bullets. This here jailhouse. Go get her and fetch her back here, boy, because I got a bad feelin' you'll never get Weedon off his horse like you done Jim Bricker. Don't stand there, boy, go fetch her down here. She can stay in this cell with me."

Walt nodded and walked out into the dingy, gloomy little corridor. As he swung past the cell containing those B-Back-to-Back men, one of them moved up until his face was recognizable in the sooty light. It was Foster Babcock.

"Hodge," he said, "I owe you an apology for all I been thinkin' about you. We all do. None of us really figured you was tellin' the truth out there in the roadway. Not until we heard Wheeler's explanation."

Walt looked in at Babcock, at those other men for a moment, then pushed on past without saying a word.

Up ahead in the doorway, Andy Blevins and the doctor were in solemn conversation. When Walt came up, even those two looked gravely at him.

Blevins said: "We heard what Fred told you. It's the truth, too. You'll never be able to take Mike like you took Jim Bricker."

"You're not up to it," murmured the doctor, considering Walt with his professional appraisal. "One body can absorb just so much punishment, Mister Hodge. The town's everlastingly grateful to you for preventing warfare right here in our roadway, but none of us would ask you to make any additional sacrifice."

"Sacrifice, hell," growled Walt, irritated by the unctuous and sepulchral tones of the medical man. "Doc, you just clean up your instruments, get some beds ready, and keep your head down."

Walt pushed past into the outer office. Andy Blevins, back there by the door, smiled bleakly and left the physician's side to collar a lounging townsman, and whisper into this man's ear to go up to the Dallas House and fetch back two bottles of whiskey. Andy gave the man a hard shove toward the door as he turned to hear Walt speak to the others in that room.

"If Weedon's coming here to finish Wheeler as we've been told, I think we just might arrange a welcoming committee for him. What do you fellows say?"

The posse men answered up, tart and loud, with Andy Blevins's bull-bass voice rising solidly and fiercely over the others. Every man there was willing and ready!

CHAPTER SIXTEEN

Over by the cell-block door the doctor stood in thoughtful silence watching Walt. Finally he went over and without a word lifted Walt's badly swollen left hand.

"Broken," he said. "Mister Hodge, you have two broken knuckles."

That hand throbbed each time Walt moved it. He glared at the medical man, drew the hand away, and said: "Never mind me, Doc. I'm not left-handed, anyway. Just do like I said . . . get some beds ready and get your tools ready."

"But you can't . . ."

"Doctor, if I let you set this hand and bandage it, Weedon would know at once I was one-handed now. I don't want to give him that satisfaction."

Walt turned toward the other men. As he started to speak, a cowboy stumped into the room with a broad grin and a bottle of rye whiskey in each fist. He solemnly walked up, put one of those bottles down next to Walt, turned, and handed the other one to Andy Blevins.

The men smiled as Andy unscrewed the cap, threw back his head, and drank. He made a growl deep in his throat, handed the bottle to the next man, and turned, both eyes copiously watering, to say to Walt: "That's real Irish whiskey . . . it's got to be, nothing could be that green and raw without bein' Irish."

Walt took a drink, twisted, and pushed the bottle toward the medical man. "Good for the blood," he said. "Have a drink, then take one to Fred Wheeler."

The whiskey made no noticeable difference among those posse men, unless it was to loosen their tongues a little.

One man said: "I figure we ought to ambush 'em when they ride in."

Another disagreed with this, saying he thought they all ought to get a-horseback, rush out, and engage Weedon beyond the town.

Walt waited for the talk to diminish before selecting a man, giving him instructions to go get atop some southward building and keep watch until he saw riders approaching, then hustle back and let Walt know. The posse man nodded and at once departed.

This quiet, efficient handling of an important factor they had otherwise overlooked silenced the others. Walt then sent another man to the livery barn with orders to locate Leila Bricker and return her to the jailhouse.

After that he considered the remaining posse men. There were several of them quite advanced in age. These men he told to remain where they were—in the jailhouse—and see that no one disturbed Wheeler or the prisoners. After making these dispositions he took one final pull at the whiskey bottle, stood up off the edge of a table he'd been perching upon, and looked around at Andy Blevins.

"What we need next," he said calmly, "is something to eat and a gallon of cold water for me."

Blevins's mouth dropped open. Those others crowding the little room also seemed nonplussed.

Walt made a crooked little smile and shrugged. "Well, until our sentinel tells us trouble's arriving, should we eat or sit around looking glum?"

He headed for the door, threw it open, and stepped out where afternoon's hurting brilliance was beginning to turn from brassy yellow to reddish yellow. Heat rolled up at him from the roadway bearing with it sharp odors and the metallic taste of dust.

He led off toward a café upon the opposite roadside and failed to notice the man he'd sent for Leila Bricker returning toward the jailhouse with her. Andy Blevins saw though, and tipped Leila a grave little bow before he too joined all the other men in trailing on across to the café.

Sunflower evidently knew what was in the wind. Very likely that messenger who Blevins had told to go buy himself a drink had done just that, and had spilled his information around up at the Dallas House. One thing was obvious, people were remaining indoors again as they had when word of Bricker's approach toward town had earlier turned them cautious and fearful.

As Andy crowded in to drop down alongside Walt at the café's long counter, he commented on this. Walt nodded, seemingly disinterested. He called his order to the café man along with all the other orders and watched the café man begin to move with inordinate speed.

"Leila's at the jailhouse," said Andy. "I just saw her go in."

Walt heeded this remark from Blevins, looked at his bad left hand which he was sheltering close to his chest, and said: "I reckon she'll talk to her father." He straightened up as the café man came over, put down a pitcher of water with a glass, then walked away again. Walt drank two glasses down without stopping. The third glass he held cupped in his right hand and said to Blevins: "Andy, you know Weedon and his bunch . . . how do you think it's going to be when he rides in?"

Blevins looked thoughtful before he answered, saying: "Mister Hodge, no man ever knows another man that well. A fellow may think he does, but he really doesn't. If you want me to guess, I'd say Weedon figures he's got this town buffaloed. He'll come in like he owns the place and the first man that drops his right hand to his holster will trigger the whole thing. One thing you *won't* be able to do is badger him like you did Bricker. He's got no particular grudge against you like Bricker had, so he'll just let you . . ."

"He's got a grudge against me, Andy. I made a fool out of him the first day I hit town. He was waiting at the Variety House to jump Bricker with his whole crew and I spoiled that. Then I saw those men of his trying to finish Bricker's range boss. I'm the only witness against them. Weedon's got plenty of reason to want me dead, all right."

Andy scowled at the platter of food the café man dumped in front of him, waited until Walt and the others roundabout had also been served, then he said: "I reckon the thing we got to do, then, is get the drop on him. Maybe like someone said over at Wheeler's office . . . ambush him."

"Maybe," mumbled Walt, beginning to wolf down his meal.

All the rumbling conversation in the café suddenly died out. Men fell to eating. For some little time, the clatter of utensils, dishes, and cups was the only considerable sound. Behind them, the café's roadside door opened and jarred closed. Some of the posse men turned. Walt and Andy Blevins were among them. The man standing over there was the one Walt had sent out to watch the southward range.

He said: "They're comin', boys. Six of 'em, and they look to be armed for bear."

"How far?" Andy Blevins asked.

"Mile, maybe a mile and a half. Ridin' along easy-like. Maybe take 'em another thirty minutes to get here." That messenger let his gaze roam up and down that counter full of men before holding his eyes steadily upon Walt as though awaiting some order.

The others also hung there watching Walt and waiting.

Andy Blevins forked up another big mouthful of food before arising. All along the counter the others took their cue from Andy and also stood up.

As Walt came up, he said to that messenger: "Go over and join the boys at the jailhouse. Stay in there. Tell them to bar the door and not to let a soul in unless it's one of us."

The messenger ducked back and went trotting away. They could distinctly hear his footfalls in the roadway hush.

"Let's go," Walt said, leading on out of the café. The last man to leave was the café man. It had taken him a moment to remove his apron, duck out back for his shotgun, and afterward to close and lock his roadside door. He was still wearing bedroom slippers but seemed to have entirely forgotten this as he went loping along after the others.

Nor was the café man the only one who stepped forth from a place of business. There was also a grocer wearing a derby hat, sleeve garters of an outrageous pink hue, and a blue pin-striped shirt. This man was also lugging a shotgun.

Walt hiked along to the southernmost edge of town before halting, turning to consider his followers, then saying to Andy Blevins they'd picked up another half-dozen men.

Andy looked and grunted. "Can't very well make 'em go back, but there's some here I don't want standin' behind me if some shootin' commences."

Walt didn't believe Weedon would be foolish enough to provoke a fight with the odds so overwhelmingly against him and said so.

Blevins simply turned, put a glum gaze out over the southward range, and said nothing. He'd already given his appraisal of Mike Weedon. His expression now told Walt he had not altered it, odds or no odds.

The men milled and murmured. A few, the original posse men Andy had selected and who had stood fast in the face of Jim Bricker's threat, examined their weapons with little talk. These were the men Walt meant to rely upon if worse came to worst, so he faced those men and addressed them: "Half of you walk west across the roadway. The other half of you stay here on the east side."

The men started to obey, but one older man stood fast. This one said to Walt: "You can't get away with it twice, Mister Hodge, if you and

Andy are figurin' to brace 'em from the center of the roadway."

Walt remembered this man grumbling a dissent before their other confrontation.

"I don't expect Weedon's going to pay much attention to me if I'm hid behind a barrel," he dryly said. "Go take your place."

The dissenter shuffled away as he'd done before, wearing the identical expression of dour misgiving.

Those additional armed townsmen were like sheep. Neither Walt nor Andy had told them what to do. Some of them aligned themselves with the posse men, some of them simply stood around doing nothing, and several of them, probably the same ones who had deserted Fred Wheeler when the fearful smell of battle was this close, simply turned and hastened away.

Walt watched these deserters, so did Andy, but neither of them said anything. There were close to twenty-five armed men sealing off any forcible entrance into Sunflower. That appeared to be more than enough to halt six cattlemen no matter how rugged Mike Weedon and his bunch might be.

Afternoon was now well advanced. Heat still lay in shimmering layers over the valley, the encircling, glazed-over mountains, and the way it reflected bitterly off particles of mica in the heavy atmosphere made men squint their eyes nearly closed, and yet it seemed to be less furiously hot than it had been two hours before in this same roadway. At least it seemed that way to Walt as he stood out there with Andy Blevins, waiting for Weedon's bunch to come up out of the dancing distance.

Normally visibility would have permitted those watchers to sight riders five miles out, but this was midsummer with all its deceptive heat haze and eye-stinging obscurity. Now, they would not see Weedon until he was within rifle range.

"It's the damned waiting," grumbled Andy, as he flicked away sweat from his nose and chin. "I remember in the war . . . it was the waitin'. Sometimes you'd see brave men wound so tight with the waitin' they'd just drop to their knees and commence blubberin' like kids."

Walt kept looking far out and saying nothing. He too felt the strain but he knew from experience that talking about it, speculating on what could happen, audibly or inaudibly, eventually got to a man and turned his resolve watery and made his legs tremble.

Although he seldom smoked and did not actually now feel any need for a cigarette, he said: "Andy, you got the makings?"

Andy had, so the two of them began working up their cigarettes. Walt had trouble with his left hand and swore irritably before he got the job finished. He leaned into Andy's match and lit up.

Andy was clumsily solicitous. "You should've let the sawbones wrap that hand."

Walt shrugged, shoved the badly discolored and twice its normal size hand inside his shirt front. Not until he'd done this did he realize he was not wearing Wheeler's badge. He thought of sending someone after his torn shirt for the badge, but he didn't. If twenty-five willing guns wouldn't deter Mike Weedon, that little steel circlet wouldn't either, he decided.

He was concentrating upon settling his broken hand in place, working the wrist so that the hand was supported, and for this little time was paying no attention to the onward country, when Andy Blevins spoke quietly at his side.

"Here they come," Andy said. "But as near as I can see from here . . . all six of 'em ain't out there."

Others among the watchers had also sighted riders emerging from the dancing distance. Those others spoke a little back and forth from their positions upon opposing sides of the southward roadway.

Walt looked, made out shimmering man shapes out there atop walking horses, and noticed that Weedon's riders were not coming in a closed-up bunch but were instead riding at least a hundred yards apart in an abreast line.

"Skirmish order," muttered Andy, likening that

approach to an army advance. "I told you, Mister Hodge, Mike Weedon ain't straightforward like old Jim Bricker."

"That's not what's interesting me right now," said Walt. "What I want to know is where those other three are."

He looked right and left beyond those riders out there, found nothing, and turned completely around to gaze back up the rearward roadway. Every other man down there with him was intently watching the onward men, and of them all only Andy Blevins heard Walt sigh. Andy turned then too.

"Quiet as you please," murmured Walt, looking straight up the rearward roadway where Mike Weedon, Charley Murchison, and George Finster were dismounting casually at the hitch rack in front of the Variety House.

"Quiet as you please, Andy."

Blevins's body jerked. His hands upon his rifle, held low, whitened at the knuckles. "Should've expected something like this," he growled, staring bitterly up where Weedon and his companions stepped up onto the plank walk, paused to look southward, laughed, and crossed on over to pass from sight into the saloon.

"I told you he wasn't like Jim Bricker, Mister Hodge." Andy raised his voice as he swung his head from left to right. "Three of 'em just entered the Variety House," he informed the other watchers. "Came around behind us and come into town from the north."

Men whirled, sensing something perilous in Weedon's trick, but there was nothing to be seen up there but three tied horses quietly drooping in the sun blast. Men muttered back and forth.

Andy swung, still frowning with humiliation, with indignation, to await word from Walt.

"Take these three," said Walt, squaring back around, facing those other Weedon riders who were slowing now less than a hundred feet out, their faces utterly devoid of expression, their eyes jumping from man to man among the watchers.

CHAPTER SEVENTEEN

Walt let those onward range riders get up to within twenty feet of him before he said to them: "That'll do, boys. That's far enough. Get down and shed your guns." He said this in an almost conversational tone of voice. There was no menace in his tone or his appearance.

Those three cowboys sat up there watching him, weighing him in their minds. Not a one of them made any move to obey.

Andy Blevins glowered. His lips were sucked back flat against his teeth. Very clearly, Andy was teetering upon the knife edge of violence, holding himself in check with great control.

"Yeah?" murmured one of Weedon's riders. "And who're you to be givin' us orders, Hodge?"

"Acting deputy sheriff until Fred Wheeler's back on his feet after being gunned down by your outfit."

"He gave us no choice, and, badge or no badge, no man's got to stand there and be shot at."

Blevins started to growl a reply to this statement. Walt silenced him with a word. On either side of them the posse men were once more aligned, ready and willing.

"It'll be up to the law courts to decide whether you boys were justified in shooting Wheeler or not. All I'm concerned with here and now is that you get down off those horses and shed your guns."

When he finished saying this, Walt half turned, looked up the roadway toward the Variety House, saw nothing up there, and faced around again.

"Spit or close the window," he said, his voice roughening toward those three men. "Get down like I said, or make your play."

"Brave, ain't you?" said that same softly drawling cowboy. "Brave as hell with a little army around you, Hodge."

This was Les Upton with the bandaged right hand.

"Are you goin' to get down?" Walt said, ignoring his comment.

"And if we don't?"

Andy Blevins had had enough. Without a word he started for that horseman holding his rifle in one hand, swinging his free hand upward and outward to drag that man off his saddle.

"Easy, blacksmith," another of those three said. This man was sitting up there with his left hand holding his reins high and in plain sight. His right hand, though, was lying in his lap.

It was this hand that lifted the slightest bit so that Blevins could see it. Andy stopped stock still. That cowboy, still with his holstered six-gun in plain sight, was pointing a small .41 under-

and-over Derringer straight at the blacksmith.

The Weedon man smiled a little as Blevins stopped moving.

"That's better," he said. "That's a lot better, blacksmith. Now just step back over where you were."

Andy didn't move though. He dropped his arm and glared, but he did not obey that soft-spoken order.

Walt, guessed what had transpired although neither he nor any of his men could see that little gun.

"Mister," Walt said to the Weedon cowboy, "you pull that trigger and you'll be dead before you hit the ground."

The third cowboy, silent up until now, said: "Hodge, you gimme proof you're legally deputized and I won't buck you. We was told Wheeler was out of it and he was the only law hereabouts."

Walt considered this man. He was younger than the others, spare of build and solemn now. Walt remembered him from that time in the Variety House when he'd met all these men.

"I'm no liar," he said to this younger one. "Deputy Wheeler appointed me to act for him after he was shot."

"Then where's the badge?"

Walt was annoyed with himself for not sending after Wheeler's badge now, but it was too late for recriminations so he said: "It's lyin' up in the roadway where I left it."

That first cowboy sneered. "Likely," he said. "Maybe you ain't a liar, Hodge, but you're sure workin' up to become one with a yarn like that."

This man straightened in his saddle, cast a sideways glance down into Andy Blevins's wrathful countenance, and said: "Why would a lawman leave his badge lyin' in the roadway?"

"It's on my shirt back there," stated Walt. "The shirt was torn after my fight with Jim Bricker."

All those three men suddenly fixed Walt with their wondering eyes. The man with the hide-out Derringer said: "You fought Jim Bricker?"

"And whipped him to a frazzle," growled Andy. "Just like I'm goin' to do to you."

The leader of Weedon's three riders frowned faintly. For the first time his expression was doubtful.

"Where's Bricker now?" he asked.

"In jail with his crew," replied Walt. "The doctor's with him."

Once more those three cowboys turned quiet briefly. Finally, that youngest man swung out and down. "That's good enough for me," he said to his companions, his voice strong with finality. "I told you fellows at the ranch there'd be another lawman around here. Downin' ol' Wheeler wasn't the end of nothing, even though Mike said it would be. It's just the beginnin'. And I'll be damned if I'm buskin' the law for any twenty a month and found."

The other two horsemen exchanged a look. The foremost one swung toward Walt. "Tell you what," he said in an altered tone of voice. "You show us Jim Bricker in jail and me and my friend here'll drop out of the game right now."

Walt nodded. "Get down and come along." He paused, saw Andy's fierce glare at one of those men, and added: "Keep your guns and don't do anything foolish." As he turned, he said over one shoulder: "Come on, Andy, never mind the hide-out pistol for now."

The five men started forward, while Weedon's men, leading their horses and walking close to one another, watched the townsmen close in behind them.

The spokesmen among them said to Walt: "Mike never figured on this. He said we'd have a little fun in Sunflower, then ride on up to B-Back-to-Back and settle Bricker's score. He sure never figured Bricker would be here in Sunflower . . . in jail."

Walt had nothing to say to those men until, just outside the jailhouse, he halted to face them.

"I'm going to tell you here and now, boys, after you've seen Bricker and his crew in their cell, you're not going to walk back out of this jailhouse."

Weedon's men looked at one another, looked

at all those grim-faced men around them, said nothing, and stalked forward.

Walt called out to the inside men, waited until the door swung open, then stepped back.

Weedon's riders walked in and at once six-guns bristled in the hands of those jailhouse guards. Andy Blevins growled for the guards to ease off. He then trailed along behind Walt and those three cowboys into the cell-block. There, Weedon's men saw Jim Bricker sitting up, looking as though he'd been mauled by a bear, and around him all his imprisoned riders.

In the adjoining cell Deputy Wheeler was also sitting up. He and the doctor were playing cards by the feeble light of a solitary candle. Wheeler squinted at those three cowboys, let off a rough curse, and called to Walt.

"Where's Mike?"

"Haven't got him yet. We're going after him now," responded Walt as he faced Weedon's men. "Now shed those guns," he ordered, and this time there was no hesitation.

Andy Blevins moved up beside one of those three, pushed his scarred face up close, and growled: "Give me that damned popgun you carry, cowboy. I'm goin' to make you eat it."

Walt interceded here, saying: "Come on, Andy. Fetch that little pistol along, we might need it."

He and Andy returned to the outer office which was now crowded with armed men.

"Lock those three up and get the doc over here," ordered Walt as he threaded his way to the door. He was speaking to the jailhouse guards. They growled that they would do this, that in fact because there were only two of those little strap-steel cages and Fred Wheeler was occupying one, they'd throw Weedon's men in with Bricker's men.

Andy Blevins smiled broadly. Clearly, Andy thought Bricker's men would give Weedon's riders a good hiding.

As the posse men left the jailhouse again, this time turning left in the wake of Walt, Blevins's former good spirits had completely returned. He grinned as the mob of armed men trooped northward toward the Variety House.

Walt considered what that cowboy had told him as he paced along. He thought it probably the truth. Certainly the cowboy had no reason to lie. Furthermore, the abrupt surrender of that youngest rider tended to verify the other man's statement that Weedon had no idea Bricker's crew was in Sunflower, that Mike Weedon and his men meant only to briefly halt in Sunflower, have a few drinks, swagger a little and buffalo the town, before striking out for the northerly range and Bricker's place to continue their feud.

He thought this accounted for Weedon's derisive laugh as he'd entered the saloon a little while before, with his henchmen Murchison and Finster. He'd seen those armed townsmen, had viewed them contemptuously after the way some of those same men had turned tail and fled during the shoot-out when Wheeler had been shot, and was now going ahead with his notion of roughing up the town a little before riding to his rendezvous with B-Back-to-Back.

As Hodge slowed his onward approach to the saloon where Weedon, George Finster, and Charley Murchison were, he wondered what it would take to disarm those three.

Andy Blevins pushed up through the crowd of armed men at Walt's back, stopped, squinted ahead where the Variety House loomed ominously quiet, and shook his head at Walt.

"This'll be chancy," Andy commented. "If you want, I'll take some of the boys and stake out the back of the place."

Walt considered this and agreed with it, but made one change. "Let someone else take the back alley watch," he said. "You stick with me, Andy."

Blevins turned, spoke roughly and rapidly, and at once half that armed body melted away toward the back alley. Then Blevins frowned at the saloon's front entrance and said: "It's awful quiet, Mister Hodge. Mike's no simpleton."

Walt also considered the empty, silent roadway up in front of the Variety House. It was as Andy had observed, entirely peaceful appearing without anyone in view. In fact, the only movement anywhere around, was where those three saddled horses stood drowsily at the rack occasionally flicking at flies with their tails.

"It's goin' to be Big Casino," murmured Blevins. "I feel it in my bones. The toughest three are in there."

Walt, thinking back to his first day in Sunflower, recalled bitter-lipped Mike Weedon, stocky George Finster, and lanky, slow-moving Charley Murchison. Of the three, he recalled Charley as a man he could have liked.

Regardless of the kind of a jackpot Charley had allowed Weedon to lead him into now, he'd struck Walt as a fair kind of a hand. He knew every trail drive, every cow camp. Every cow town had at least one Charley Murchison—likeable men, resourceful, fearless, too susceptible to strong leadership perhaps, too easily influenced, but not inherently bad or vicious. Walt felt a little sorry for Charley because, although he did not say it, he felt as Andy did. This wasn't going to be any face down as it had been with those other three. Neither was it going to resolve into a personal feud as the fight with Bricker's B-Back-to-Back had.

Andy broke in upon Walt's thoughts, saying: "We got five men here with shotguns, Walt. You figurin' on marchin' right up into the saloon?"

"Yes."

"Then let's take them fellows along. One thing . . . most men will make a rush for their guns when other fellows got the same armament, but no sane man will try to draw a six-gun against a shotgun the width of a saloon."

Walt turned, held out a hand toward that carpet-slippered café man, and said: "Loan me your scatter-gun." When the café cook extended the weapon, Walt took it. As he bent to examine it, he said to Andy: "Get another one. No sense in more than just you and me going in there when they've got six-guns and we've got these things."

Andy took a shotgun, frowned, and wagged his head back and forth. Clearly, Andy was not enthusiastic.

CHAPTER EIGHTEEN

Walt straightened up with his shotgun. He ran a careful look on ahead. There still was no sound, no movement, coming from up at the Variety House. He pictured the bitter face of Mike Weedon as he lounged up against the bar in there waiting for his three tough cowboys to come stalking in, laughing over having cowed that knot of townsmen south of town.

"Weedon will be ready," he murmured to Andy at his side. "He may think the town's quaking in its boots . . . but he'll be ready."

Andy started to speak. Walt turned, cut across Andy's words, and said to those remaining posse men: "Go over across the road and take positions. If there's shooting, stay out of the saloon until Andy and I come out. If we *don't* come out . . . just wait until Weedon does, and cut him down. You understand?"

The men muttered understanding and soft protest at the same time.

Walt faced away from them, shot Andy a look, and started forward.

One of those men posted to the opposite plank walk suddenly stopped out in the roadway's center, stooped to scoop up something, then turned and trotted back.

Andy saw this man approaching, muttered a curse of annoyance, and halted. Walt also halted. That posse man came up, handed Walt Fred Wheeler's badge, and turned to rush on across where his friends were beginning to position themselves along the plank walk, facing resolutely westward toward the Variety House.

Walt gazed a moment at Wheeler's badge, then pinned it upon his shirt front. He seemed sardonic about this, and Blevins, seeing that expression, said: "It might deflect a slug even if it doesn't do anythin' else."

The two of them strolled on again.

They were within thirty feet of the saloon's bat-wing doors when thick-set George Finster strolled out. George was gazing southward toward the far end of town and did not immediately sight Walt and the blacksmith approaching. In fact, he saw those men opposite the saloon first, saw their arms and their tough-set faces. George drew up a little.

Walt plainly saw surprise shadow his features. Obviously, like the other three Weedon cowboys, George had believed what Mike had evidently said about Sunflower being cowed after the shooting of Fred Wheeler.

Suddenly, George caught movement from the edge of his eye and swung. That was when he saw Walt and Andy Blevins standing there no more than thirty feet away.

For a second those three men looked steadily at one another. George's gaze dropped to those double-barreled scatter-guns. His right hand was hanging loosely at his side. Walt saw it crook the slightest bit at the elbow, hoisting Finster's fingers to within inches of his saw-handled Colt.

"Don't do it," Walt warned Finster, but he was a fraction of a second too late.

George let off a snarl, dropped down, and blurred for his six-gun. Andy Blevins fired first, Walt second. That initial cluster of birdshot lifted stocky George Finster off his feet. The second full charge knocked him over backward in a heap ten feet away.

From within the saloon came the quick, discordant sound of glass breaking, probably some drink dropped from a startled hand.

Walt jumped sideways to land with both shoulders against the front of a store. Andy was moving too, but a six-gun roared from the saloon window, shattering glass and plowing up a foot-long splinter from the plank walk under Blevins's churning boots. Andy covered the last five feet in one big bound.

Walt, with just one charge left in that shotgun, saw that pistol barrel up there through the smashed window, but did not fire at it.

Gradually, silence returned.

Across the roadway, at the first blasts, those positioned posse men faded from sight. Some hugged back deeply in recessed doorways, others had sprung inside stores and were crouched there now, watching and waiting. Others had simply dropped from sight altogether. Most of these would appear later at upstairs windows and upon roof tops, but immediately after the killing of George Finster there were only two men visible the full width and length of Main Street, and those two were flattened up out of sight of Charley Murchison and Mike Weedon, unless those two left the saloon.

Andy's choppy breathing was audible even before he murmured to Walt he wished they'd taken more shotgun shells when they'd appropriated those guns. Walt agreed with this, but kept intently watching the front of the yonder saloon as he spoke.

It was a nerve-racking time. Walt had not counted on Finster walking out like that. Now, he thought that perhaps he should have anticipated something, though, because the lounging men inside the saloon were bound to wonder about their companions after enough time had passed.

Suddenly there was a quick rush of gunfire around behind the Variety House.

Blevins warned Walt: "They tried to slip out the back way, by golly."

Walt kept silent, assessing that furious shooting, then decided to gamble that Andy was right. He jumped away from the wall at his back and started swiftly forward. Andy, caught unprepared by this movement, was slower in reaching the Variety House's roadside front wall, but he made it. He positioned himself next to the shattered window behind Walt.

For a moment longer that firing continued around back. Walt dropped down, raised up for a fast look in, saw a man backing away and facing toward the building's rear exit. Walt ducked from sight, darted over to the bat-wing doors, and was poised to spring inside when a gunshot from behind, across the roadway, struck one of those doors breaking out several louvers and bringing that man in there whipping around. He threw an unsighted shot outward and more louvers fell.

Andy, still over by the window, saw those two slugs wreck the door and swung, a snarl upon his face, as he sought to find the posse man who had fired that first shot. There was no one in sight anywhere.

Walt had flinched from the first bullet and jumped back when the answering slug had burst out of the saloon. He pressed up flat against the outside wall, waiting. It occurred to him that only one man was now inside. The other one, either Charley or Mike Weedon, must have stopped lead in the attempted break-out into the rear alleyway.

Walt held his scatter-gun high across his body with both hands, looked southward where Andy was crouched at the window, and let the silence settle dustily again before he called out to that man inside.

"Throw out your gun! You haven't the chance of a snowball in hell. Throw out your gun and call it off!"

No answer came back to this.

Walt and Andy exchanged a look. Andy's face was shiny with sweat and smoothed out from tension and turmoil. His eyes were screwed up nearly closed although this eastward side of Main Street was by now, this late in the afternoon, solidly shaded.

"Toss it out, damn you!" growled Blevins from his crouched position by the ruined window. "Pardner, you don't have a prayer of livin' through this if you don't."

A muffled voice called back: "And I don't have a prayer if I do, either. I seen those damned townsmen out there with their shotguns and rifles."

Walt spoke up next. "Toss out your gun and stay in there until I come for you."

No gun sailed out.

Once again Walt exchanged a glance with Andy Blevins. The blacksmith's shirt was dark with perspiration, not all of it inspired by the breathless heat though. Andy was as tightly wound as a coiled spring.

"Who's out there?" that surviving member of Weedon's crew asked.

198

"Hodge and Blevins," Walt replied. "Do as I say and you'll make it all right."

"Sure you will," growled Andy. "You'll live to hang, Weedon. It's long overdue for you too."

"This isn't Mike!" called out that besieged man. "This here is Charley Murchison."

Walt felt relief although he wasn't certain just why he should. He yelled: "Where's Weedon? We want him worst of all."

"You got him," said Charley. "You wanted him the worst way, Hodge, and that's how you're goin' to get him. Weedon stopped a head-on blast from somebody's shotgun at the back door from less than fifty feet. He's lyin' back there. Dead as can be."

"Then," said Walt, "you're all that's left, Charley. Throw out the gun and stay right where you are."

Another agonizing moment dragged past for those two exposed men along the saloon's front wall. Andy flung sweat off his face, rippled his jaw muscles at the agony of remaining crouched for so long, and moved his lips in a silent curse Walt could read all the way over where he stood waiting.

A six-gun sailed over the bat-wing doors, struck hard upon the plank walk, bounced out into roadway dust, and lay there shining dully in the shifting sunlight.

"Any more?" called out Walt. "Any hide-outs, Charley?"

"No! I'm plumb unarmed in here, Hodge. Feel plumb naked right about now."

Walt cocked his shotgun, stepped through the broken doors, and halted.

Charley Murchison was standing with his back to the deserted bar, both hands over his head. His face was gray, its expression full of doubt and moving uncertainty. He looked away from Walt's twin-barreled riot-gun only when Andy also pushed inside and halted.

"Go look him over," Walt said to the blacksmith. He waited until Andy had roughly checked Murchison for other weapons, then jerked his head rearward. "Tell the others it's all over, Andy. Tell them no more shooting. I'll stay in here until you're sure it'll be safe to bring Charley out."

Blevins strode from the saloon. Moments later his bull-bass voice could be heard all over town profanely pronouncing that the fighting was over.

Walt said: "Turn around, Charley."

Murchison obeyed. Those two looked long at one another.

Charley said with a wag of his head: "I told Mike you were no one to fool with."

Walt ignored that. "Who shot Bricker's range boss? Was it Les Upton?" he demanded.

"George Finster. He didn't mean to hit him,

though. We just wanted him to clear out so's we could finish pushing the cattle up north."

"Then why shoot at all?"

Charley's eyes narrowed. "I'll tell you why. You didn't know Carl Hathaway, Hodge. He was plenty mean when he was roiled. You couldn't *talk* him into doin' anything. That's why we fired. Afterward, George said he thought he'd tilted his muzzle plenty high, when Carl went riding away."

Walt considered this. Some of it made sense, even though so much of what had happened was senseless. He remembered how Carl had struck him without warning. He could believe that part about Carl being hard to convince. The shooting made sense too. Many a man had tilted his muzzle to fire over a distant man's head, forgetting entirely to take into account that the bullet would drop steadily lower as it sped along.

Blevins poked his head through the doorway. "Walt, it's safe to bring him out now. But if he acts foolish . . . so help me, I'll be the first one to fire."

Walt gestured with the shotgun. Charley started across the room. At the doorway, as he looked out, he saw all those grim faces and armed men; drawing in a quick breath, before he took a big step, and was outside upon the plank walk.

Walt moved in behind him, gave Charley a light nudge with the shotgun, and herded him down to the jailhouse. There, with a converging crowd of armed men thickening around them, Walt drove the last of Mike Weedon's men inside, past the flinty-faced jailhouse guards and on into the cell-block.

As Fred Wheeler watched them file in, he called out the same question he'd asked before: "Walt, where's Weedon?"

"Dead," Walt answered, biting that one word off as he waited for Andy to open the adjoining cell which was now crammed full of dejected men.

"You get him?" Wheeler asked.

"No, Fred, it wasn't me. There was so much shooting going on around back it's difficult to say who really got him."

At these words, Leila materialized from among those incarcerated men. Blevins held the door for her to come out, then slammed it closed with savage finality, and stood there glaring in at those thoroughly beaten and demoralized cow-men.

Walt put aside his shotgun, held out his right hand to Leila, and walked with her out of the cell-block.

Blevins turned to speak as his eyes followed those two, but head-bandaged, old Fred Wheeler growled at him: "Andy, you fool, they don't want you traipsin' along. Go get me a mop or something with a handle I can use to reach through the bars with and use to prod hell out of Jim Bricker."

Andy looked around at Fred with a screwed-up expression. "Huh?" he grunted. "What?"

"You heard me, confound you. Get me something with a long handle . . . broom, mop, I don't care. Need to thump Bricker with. All the time that fighting was going on out there he was saying he'd give anything if he could just undo all the harm he's caused. Well, I can't get up yet and neither can he, but until we can, I want to see him get what he's got coming. The only regret I got is that Mike Weedon isn't here, too. He's even more responsible for this mess than Bricker is."

Andy Blevins turned and slowly walked up out of the dingy cell-block. He arrived in the outer office just in time to see the roadside door close behind Walt Hodge and Leila Bricker.

One of the men in that stuffy, crowded little office turned and softly said: "Andy, she's taken him somewhere to care for the hand he busted on her pa's thick skull. Ain't that touchin'?"

Andy dropped down upon a wall bench, exhausted from the strain, and said: "Yeah, it's so touchin' I need another snort of that whiskey. Where in tarnation is it? You boys haven't plumb drunk it all up, have you?"

Someone produced a nearly emptied bottle and handed it timidly to the blacksmith.

As Andy tilted his head and lifted the bottle one of the posse men said a little indignantly: "Well, hell, Andy, least you could do for the fellow that turned this here gun town back into our village of Sunflower is offer up a toast for him."

Andy lowered his head, gazed owlishly around, solemnly nodded, and declared: "Here's to the newly-weds. He's the only fellow I ever knew whipped his pappy-in-law to a fare-thee-well *before* he married the girl."

He tipped up the bottle, drank deeply, set it down, and belched wetly. "Any man ever says a word . . . even so much as a whisper . . . against Walt Hodge while I'm able, and so help me I'll crush his skull like an egg!"

"Amen, Andy, Amen."

About the Author

Lauran Paine, who has written over a thousand books, was born in Duluth, Minnesota. His family moved to California when he was at a young age and his apprenticeship as a Western writer came about through the years he spent in the livestock trade, rodeos, and even motion pictures where he served as an extra because of his expert horsemanship in several films starring movie cowboy Johnny Mack Brown. In the late 1930s, Paine trapped wild horses in northern Arizona and, for a time, even worked as a professional farrier. Paine came to know the Old West through the eyes of many who had been born in the 19th Century, and he learned that Western life had been vastly different from the way it was portrayed on the screen. "I knew men who had killed other men," he later recalled. "But they were the exceptions. Prior to and during the Depression, people were just too busy eking out an existence to indulge in Saturday-night brawls." He served in the U.S. Navy in the Second World War and began writing for Western pulp magazines following his discharge. It is interesting to note that his earliest novels were published in the British market and he soon had as strong a following in that country as in the United States. Paine's Western fiction is characterized by strong plots, authenticity, an apparently effortless ability to construct situation and character, and a preference for building his stories upon a solid foundation of historical fact. *Adobe Empire* (1956), one of his best novels, is a fictionalized account of the last twenty years in the life of trader William Bent and, in an off-trail way, has a melancholy, bittersweet texture that is not easily forgotten. In later novels like *The White Bird* (1997) and *Cache Cañon* (1998), he showed that the special magic and power of his stories and characters had only matured along with his basic themes of changing times, changing attitudes, learning from experience, respecting Nature, and the yearning for a simpler, more moderate way of life.

Center Point Large Print
600 Brooks Road / PO Box 1
Thorndike, ME 04986-0001 USA

(207) 568-3717

US & Canada:
1 800 929-9108
www.centerpointlargeprint.com

3 1333 05046 4369